THE CONGO VENUS

THE CONGO VENUS

MATTHEW HEAD

PERENNIAL LIBRARY

Harper & Row, Publishers

New York, Cambridge, Philadelphia, San Francisco
London, Mexico City, São Paulo, Sydney

A hardcover edition of this book was first published by Simon & Schuster, in 1950. It is here reprinted by arrangement.

First PERENNIAL LIBRARY edition published 1982.

ISBN: 0-06-080597-8 (previously ISBN: 0-8240-2374-9)

82 83 84 85 10 9 8 7 6 5 4 3 2 1

PART ONE

CHAPTER ONE

First off, I want to say that this happened in the Congo, and second I want to say what Liliane Morelli looked like, because the place she lived and the way she looked were the determining factors in her life, and in her death.

Her name, Liliane Morelli, doesn't suggest her appearance. "Liliane" suggests delicacy, at least it does to me, and "Morelli" of course is Italian, so you think of a brunette, when as a matter of fact the most striking thing about her was her extreme blondness. I described her once as a "big blonde" and found that I had given an entirely false picture, suggesting a kind of deteriorating effulgence, just the reverse of her full blown but still very fresh quality. Liliane Morelli was young, in her early twenties when I first saw her, although you would never have described her as a girl, somehow. She was tall, with magnificent breasts and full hips, but she wasn't "big" in the sense that "big" suggests something ungainly or overblown. She was a wonderful-looking woman, very female—and very unwise.

I would hesitate to describe her as beautiful, because she didn't have the classical regularity of feature or the sparkle and animation that can make up for the lack of it, or any exotic quality at all, but even the people who disliked her, and there were certainly a lot of those, admitted that she was a good-looking woman, although those who disliked her most took relish in saying that she would fatten and coarsen early. But this she didn't live to do.

She looked Dutch, but she was Belgian, like her husband,

and inevitably she suggested a Rubens Venus, with the healthy luxuriance of her flesh, and the glistening silky quality of her yellow hair, and the opulence of her figure—a figure somewhat modified and trimmed down from the baroque Rubens model, it's true, but still pretty sumptuous, a female figure on the grand scale.

Her origins were obscure, and some people said she had changed her name from Gerda to Liliane in an attempt at elegance, but about this I wouldn't know. I don't know what her maiden name had been, either, but even in the case of her husband, "Morelli" is a misnomer since it was his Italian great-grandfather's name, and you wouldn't have known to look at him that Morelli had a drop of Latin blood. He was a pure Flemish type, although not a very attractive one—beefy, sweaty, pasty, and with a great sagging belly, a Rubens Hercules to his wife's Venus, but a Hercules gone soft and white in middle age. The gap between his age and Liliane's may not have been as much as twenty-five years, but it certainly wasn't much less.

So if I have established now what Liliane Morelli looked like, if I can refer to her and you can get something of the right picture, I can go ahead and talk about Dr. Mary Finney before I go ahead with the story of Liliane Morelli, because if it hadn't been for Dr. Finney, there wouldn't have been much of any story to tell about Liliane.

My good friend Dr. Mary Finney isn't much given to formal philosophical statement, and she would wither you with one good strong snort if you intimated to her that she was any kind of philosopher, formal or the kind they call homely. The most she would admit to would be that she is probably the best doctor working within two hundred miles of any point on the equator, and has been for thirty years. But as for thinking of herself as really smart, she doesn't look at it that way. Instead, she is apt to think that other people are just sort of stupid and confused, the way I am, or at least the way I seem to her much of the time. I am considered fairly bright by most people, including the ones who make out the Civil Service examinations, and my own mental processes seem to me clear as a bell, until Miss Finney explains them to me and shows me what has really been going on. To repeat something I've said before, she has told me that what I substitute for thinking is nothing more than the distortion of obvious fact by the systematic application of sentimental prejudice, but in the case of Liliane Morelli, Miss Finney saw eye to eye with me. That is, we agree with one another as to the kind of person she had been, and I say "had been", because Miss Finney didn't know anything much about Liliane Morelli until after Liliane Morelli had died.

Miss Finney was talking about Liliane's death when she came as close to getting philosophical, in a popular sense of the word, as she ever allowed herself to get. "I dunno, Hoopie," she said to me, "death—I've seen a lot of it, naturally, and I can't get as wrought up over it as most people do. I don't think I'm just case-hardened. Your Madame Morelli, for instance. Young, good-looking, all that—any sudden death is a shock, especially when it's somebody as full of life as you say she was, but get away from it just a little, just a few days, and you begin to see that person, really, for the first time."

"I don't get it," I said.

Miss Finney hesitated a moment and then said, "It's just that death makes a kind of frame for life." She paused again, looking a little uncomfortable at what she had said, then went on, "I mean, the minute you're dead, the minute the whole thing is finished and over with, you're a complete person for the first time. When a person's alive, your perspective on him is all out of kilter. It's like one of those snapshots that kids like to take, of somebody lying down with his feet up

5

close to the camera so you don't see anything much but feet. When a person's alive, all you really see is what's nearest you, the way they're acting or thinking at that time of their life, at that moment, even. Parts take on so much importance that they're out of balance with the whole. But when they're dead, you get off and you see the whole thing and you know them for the first time. Does that make sense?"

"I guess so."

"Of course it does. And what I'm trying to get is the whole picture of this Morelli woman."

"I don't see how you expect to get it from me. I didn't really know her well."

"You're the best I can do. I can't ask these questions of anybody else in town—not now. You give me everything you can, and I'll be able to fill in the blanks. Now go ahead. When was the next time you saw her?"

My voice was tired and fuzzy because by that time I had been talking to Miss Finney about Liliane Morelli for three hours running, but I wanted to keep on talking, because I was finding that the more I talked to Miss Finney, the more I discovered for myself.

All this was in Léopoldville, which is the capital city of the Belgian Congo. It's a fine little city, as little equatorial cities go, but it's still a little equatorial city all the same, you can't get around that. It has 6,000 whites and 60,000 or 600,000 blacks, I've read both figures, but it doesn't make much difference. There are an awful lot of them, segregated in their own tremendous village (I suppose with that many people it's a city, but somehow you can't think of a native settlement, no matter how big, as anything but a village) which has a strict curfew that says they've got to be in there by nine at night and not come out again until five the next morning. The curfew also keeps whites out for the same hours, and I have an idea that the most interesting things that happen in Léopoldville happen in there during that time.

In addition to six thousand inhabitants, the white city of Léopoldville proper has, to name a few items as they come to mind, three ice-cream parlors, two newspapers of diminutive size, two movies, one of which runs almost every night, a bunch of stores where you can usually get anything you want, provided it isn't anything you couldn't get in an American village of five hundred, a few specialty shops, a golf club, a dance-and-social-function club, and a swimming club called the Funa—all these clubs for the elite, to which I happened to belong as an American on the Government payroll—and several cafés, including one called the Equatoriale, which is where this story, in a way, begins. The rest of Léopoldville is largely consulates and residences, some of these pretty comfortable, and some fancy avenues laid out on the general scheme of Hausmann's Paris boulevards, but looking empty and self-conscious while they wait for the town to grow up to them.

The Café Equatoriale is an undistinguished little dump of a café but pleasant enough, and it was especially pleasant at this point, because to sit across any table, distinguished or undistinguished, from Mary Finney, is a treat, and this was particularly good because she had just come back to town after several months away.

It was about two weeks after the death of Liliane Morelli, and so far as I knew, Miss Finney didn't know the Morellis at all, since she only hit Léopoldville from time to time en route to or from her own stamping ground, which is the Kivu, the great mountainous country right in the heart of Africa. As for me, I hadn't thought much one way or another about Madame Morelli's death. When I first heard of it, I had an immediate sensation of regret that I hadn't known her better, and for a few days everybody talked about her with that particular sweetness they save for people who have been maligned in life, but there had been nothing unusual in the circumstances of her death except its suddenness, and even

7

this suddenness was a fairly normal aspect of death in those parts. But now, after two weeks, I had almost forgotten her, and I certainly had no idea that Miss Finney could be interested in any way whatever.

The sun was blazing outside the café, and it was hot enough even in the comparative gloom inside to keep a little film of perspiration on you, and Miss Finney's big freckled arms shone faintly in the dimmish light, although for the most part she was just a big hillocky silhouette capped by the pale dome of her sun helmet, against the merciless glare that vibrated beyond the big front window. It was early in the afternoon, and we were alone in the café. She took off the helmet long enough to tuck up a small hank of carroty hair, then settled the helmet on her head again, sighed heavily, and reached for her glass of lemon soda. She took a sip, set the glass down again, and said out of the clear sky, "Hoopie—this Morelli woman. Did you know her?"

"Morelli? Madame Morelli? Sure."

"Very well?"

"Why—I don't know. No, not very well, I guess."

"How well?"

"Oh—pretty well, I guess. Depends on what you mean by well. I saw her around a lot, and I had one long talk with her, once, but—I don't know what you're after."

"I just mean, how well? It looks like you could answer that."

I said, "What is this?" because I had learned, by this time, to keep a sharp eye on Miss Finney's questions.

She grinned at me and said, "Don't look so suspicious. My God, Hoop, I hope the U.S. Government doesn't ever put you on work that involves any kind of deception. You've got the openest goddam pan I ever saw on a boy in my life."

"Well, well," I said. "Home again."

"You didn't answer my question," Miss Finney said. "I asked you—"

8

"You didn't answer mine," I told her. "I asked you what this was."

"It's an interrogation," Miss Finney said. "In my own simple way, I happen to be an M.D., and when somebody dies out here, naturally I'm interested."

"Oh, sure, naturally," I said. "Well, let's see, there was a Portuguese storekeeper died here about three months ago, used to rent bicycles as a side-line, I remember. Want to know about him?"

"Now, Hoopie," she said.

"You're not fooling me," I said, as the best general over-all protection. "You're puzzling me, but you're not fooling me. But if you want to know, and you probably already *do* know, Liliane Morelli died of blackwater fever, oh, a couple of weeks ago, but I *sure* don't see what that has to do with how well I knew her."

Miss Finney sighed again and said, "I dunno, Hoop, sometimes it seems like life isn't worth the struggle any more. Things get more complicated all the time. You used to be so simple I could get anything I wanted out of you without half trying. Now you want to bollix everything all up by asking why this and why that. All right, I've got something up my sleeve, but I want to let it ride for a while. Is that all right?"

"It's a mixed metaphor, but otherwise I guess it's all right."

She ignored this and went on, "And I did already know it was blackwater fever."

"Well, that's all I can tell you. She had that Dr. What's-his-name, the funny one—you know, Gollmer."

"Yes, Dr. Gollmer. I knew that too."

"Oh, you did. I'm doing fine. Do you know about him? About what people say?"

"Indeed I do," Miss Finney said, "and that's mostly why I'm pumping you. Look, Hoopie, I've got some questions. I'll tell you something you don't know about Madame

9

Morelli and about Dr. Gollmer too, all in good time, but right now I'm going back to how well you knew her. I'm asking you that again."

We were sitting well toward the back of the café. Some people came in the front door and Miss Finney paused, watching them. They looked around the place, then chose a table down near the front, far enough away so that we could still talk without being heard. Miss Finney watched them until they were preoccupied with their own talk, then turned to me and said, "If there's no other way to get it out of you, I'll ask specific questions. Specifically, were you sleeping with her?"

"Was I— *What?*"

"When you force me to be specific," Miss Finney said, "I'm specific. I just thought I'd start at the top and work down. I take it you *weren't* sleeping with her."

"I certainly was not!" I said.

She went on, a little too casually, "No need to get huffy about it. You might have been. You're young. You're fairly normal, for your generation. You're in Africa, where anything goes. Also, you're adequately attractive for purposes of light entertainment, even if no one would describe you as a ball of fire. Adequately attractive for the kind of light entertainment they tell me La Morelli was preoccupied with. From what I hear," she said, raising her hand at me because I had opened my mouth to say something, "from what I hear, the Morelli woman was both desirable and available. There." She lowered her hand and said genially, "Your turn now."

"Look," I said. "For you, you're not doing well at all. I didn't think you could be so gullible. You come here talking about a woman you don't even know, probably never even saw, and right away you pick up the small-time gossip that goes on in a place like this, 'They say,' 'They tell me,' 'From what I hear,' all that stuff, and you give me the old routine about Liliane Morelli being a sure lay—"

"A what?"

"An easy make. Do you know that one?"

"I can figure it out. Go on."

"Well, anyway, you give me this stuff about her that used to go all over town all the time, when as a matter of fact I bet nobody could give you an ounce of proof, not an ounce, and if you ask me—"

Miss Finney was really beaming. "Hoop," she interrupted, "for me, I'm still doing all right. That's exactly what I wanted to know. To do what I want you to do, you've got to have liked Madame Morelli some, and I think you did. And you've got to be able to separate heresay and casual or vindictive statement from whatever kind of truth lies beneath it, and—golly, listen to me talk. Let's get out of here, let's go somewhere." She reached across the table and patted my hand, or rather pounded it a couple of times, and said, "Where do we go? So you can begin at the first. I want to know the first time you saw Liliane Morelli and all about it, and all the other times. Where to?"

"Hippo Point," I said, and we got up and I paid the check and we left.

CHAPTER TWO

Hippopotamus Point is a kind of parking overlook outside of town where a small terrace with benches and a retaining wall have been built up at the top of the cliff, the cliff that drops off into the Congo, and there is a little path near by that winds down through thickets to another couple of benches near by. There is supposed to be a hippopotamus-in-residence in the river at this point and everybody I know except me says he really has seen it, all except Mary Finney, who wouldn't even look for it, because she said that after thirty years of seeing so many of them off and on she'd take a heap more interest in the sight of a good old Kansas mule. Because Miss Finney is originally from Fort Scott, Kansas, although everybody always calls her a New England spinster just because she's never been married and because she once made a visit to Connecticut with her good New England spinster friend and fellow-worker, Miss Emily Collins. Maybe there isn't any genus Middle-Western-spinster, but that is probably what Miss Finney is, since there certainly isn't any such thing as the genus Congo-spinster.

Miss Finney and I went out to Hippopotamus Point, then, and I told her about the first time I had seen Liliane Morelli. To tell it here I have to go into a little more detail, because, for instance, I have to explain about my friend Schmitty, and other things now and then that Miss Finney already knew about:

I was in the Congo first during the war, with one of the civilian agencies, then I had a very unsensational tour in the service and then I came back to Léopoldville to do a kind of wind-up job on the contracts we had made earlier. The first time I saw Madame Morelli was early in the game, not long after my first assignment to Léopoldville. It happened to be at the same café, the little Equatoriale, that I have just been talking about, but we were sitting outside, on the concrete terrace, since it was early in the evening and the sun had dropped dead promptly at 6 P.M. the way it always does, and hence it was no cooler one place than another. It was the time of day when the heat begins to lift enough so that you feel you can breathe without actual physical effort, and the air begins to feel something like air when you take it into your lungs, instead of like soup. I was with this Schmitty friend of mine, a sub-sub-consul who was 4-F on about eight counts in addition to diplomatic exemption, and I had been admiring in an abstract kind of way a pretty brown-haired girl, sixteen years old or so, who was eating some kind of magenta-colored ice a couple of tables away. She was really quite pretty, feature by feature, although she had a discontented look that couldn't be entirely explained away by the heat, and from what I could see of her above the table, no objections at all could be made to the general arrangement of essentials. What I was trying to figure out was why she left me cold, speaking strictly metaphorically in that climate. She was with a militantly respectable-looking middle-aged woman who half suggested a duenna and half suggested a good bourgeois mamma. This woman had a very sharp eye, and she didn't like my looking at them, but I kept trying to look, dovetailing these looks in between her glances in my direction. The girl attended strictly to business, eating her ice without looking around at all, as a nice girl should, especially when accompanied by a duenna who looked as if she might crack her over the knuckles if she so much as lifted an eyelid in the direction of the vulgar fellow at the table with Schmitty.

Schmitty and I weren't engaged in anything more strenuous than the occasional bending of the elbow to raise our beers through the eighteen-inch interval between tabletop and mouth. We weren't even talking, just sitting there in the torpor that you can spend half your life in, when you're that near the equator and the humidity is trembling on the edge of a hundred and one.

But then Liliane Morelli walked in, and if there was one thing you felt around Liliane Morelli, it wasn't torpor. You might not like her, and in fact at first glance I disliked her, because she looked too big and brash; and you might not be feeling like going in for the kind of sport Miss Finney described as "light entertainment," which her figure immediately called to mind. But you didn't feel torpor. She was one of those people always called "alive," and I don't mean highly animated or sparkling. This aliveness was like an emanation from her flesh. In a tropical locality where all the women cultivated a Garboesque air of sexual languor, partly out of climatic necessity and partly because it was still modish that year, this aliveness was almost flagrant, like an offense. And I know now that a lot of Liliane Morelli's trouble came about because she had this aliveness, which was not an affectation at all, but very real, and she had no idea what to do with it or where to direct it.

She came striding across the café terrace, with at least seven or eight men trailing after her in a way that was downright suggestive. She had on shorts and a halter, I think it's called—one of those exterior bra things—in a rich, bright native print, as beautiful a native print as I have ever seen. You couldn't miss her, and she was making just about as many mistakes at one time as any woman in the Congo could manage to make. In the first place, the shorts-and-bra costume would have been wrong for her anywhere. She was good-looking, not cute, and the shorts and bra were cute, definitely. With her hair and her figure and her height she should have looked queenly, but in the costume she had chosen she just looked big and sexy and incompletely dressed. For a second mistake, she was in a town where people might go in for plenty of private unconventionalities but were always pretty careful, in their conservative Belgian way, to be completely conventional in public, and the idea of a costume like that, on anybody, not only in public but in a café at the busy evening hour, was grotesque. A couple of her men carried golf bags, which explained her costume, but it still wasn't good. In the third place, although this might not sound so bad to anyone who hasn't lived in a community where six thousand whites have to remain demigods to many times that number of natives, it was the worst kind of mistake to use that native material. It was beautiful material, much better looking than the second-rate European prints the rest of the women in the café were wearing, but the idea of a white woman wearing native fabric in a town where the color line was drawn with a rigidity that would make the most hidebound American community look free and easy—it was unheard of, that's all, and absolutely beyond the pale.

I forgot about the brown-haired girl who left me cold, and said to Schmitty, "What's *that?*"

Schmitty kept his glance on the over-generous exposure of bare thigh, and said, "That's my tragedy."

"She's a tragedy," I agreed, "but she's drawing a great house. Shall we line up?"

Schmitty put on all the air of dignity that a little balding jockey-sized double-sub-consul can assume, and said, "You can lay off the cracks. Can you imagine me in that line-up? I'd look like a Chihuahua in a bunch of Airedales." His eyes followed the group until they had gone inside the café, and only their heads and shoulders were visible as they stood at the bar. Liliane's yellow hair attracted the light as if a baby spot were playing on it. Schmitty heaved a sigh that came up all the five-feet-six from the bottoms of his shoes and repeated, "My tragedy." He added, "They're *all* my tragedy."

I asked, "Is she as easy as she looks?"

Schmitty shrugged. "So they say, so they say. Don't ask me. I'm the little boy with his nose against the candy shop window." He looked with distaste at what was left of his glass of beer and said, "I think I'll start on whisky," and called the waiter.

Maybe I'm too generous to Liliane Morelli in retrospect, feeling as I do that what happened to her was all out of proportion to her offense. It's true that she didn't have a lick of sense about appearances. She could have led the private life of a saint, but with the public indiscretions she committed, like striding up to the bar with those men, when she should at least have stayed out at the golf club, and with all the other violations of superficial convention she was guilty of—sometimes through ignorance and sometimes through carelessness —with all these violations, she could have led the private life of a saint, and things would still have happened to her as they did. She always inspired talk like Schmitty's and mine. When you first saw her you just began thinking that way, and then it got to be a habit of thought around town so that whenever her name was mentioned, somebody could be trusted to go into the same old routine. It's a truism that we tend to be what people expect of us, and in Liliane's case, at least, what they expected of her seemed obvious because of the way she looked, and she didn't manage those looks right. A lot of the life Liliane Morelli had to accept was determined more by the way she looked than by the way she might have felt and thought about things if all her relations with people hadn't had to channel themselves through the apparent sexuality of her body. I suppose I'm being pretty awkward and obvious and roundabout in an effort to say that the way we think and feel is determined a lot more by the way we look than we have any idea of. I tried to say something like this to Mary Finney.

16

"Oh, sure," she said. "Look at me. Do you think I'd be an aging female medical missionary sitting here on Hippopotamus Point at the rear end of nowhere if I'd had soft curly hair and no freckles and hadn't outweighed half the boys in town? I'd probably be the leading dowager in Fort Scott, Kansas, right now. Or maybe I'd even have got as far afield as Kansas City. I might have developed a local reputation for my angel food cake. Look here, Hoop," she snapped, "I'm enough of a sentimentalist to feel a strong prejudice in Liliane's favor, but let's not get pathetic about it. I've seen plenty of good-looking girls who managed to overcome the handicap."

"Everything I say," I complained, "you make it sound silly."

Miss Finney smiled and said, "I don't mean to. Go ahead."

"There isn't much more to it, about that first time I saw her, I mean. But first I want to say something. Sentimental or not, I think Liliane had a sweetness of nature that stood in her way."

"When did you discover that?"

"I'll tell you when I get to it. Is that all right?"

"It's the way I want it. I want to get acquainted with her the way you did. The straighter you tell it the straighter I'm apt to get it, and don't jump around any more forecasting things like this sweetness-of-nature stuff. But since you've started it, tell me one more thing: do you think she was stupid?"

"Certainly not."

"She did stupid things."

"No she didn't. She did careless things. I think she was ignorant. More than that—by golly, I think she was innocent, she had a kind of innocence. That sounds funny, but I think it's true. But she wasn't stupid."

"Well, do you think she was bright, then?"

I thought about this a minute, and then said, "No, I don't.

The more I talk to you about her, the more I learn about her, and I may change my mind, but for right now I don't think she was awfully bright. Or shrewd. That's what she wasn't —shrewd."

"Well, we'll see. Drop this now, and go on."

"That's all there is to that incident, except the little bit about the brown-haired girl."

"You mean the cold-leaving brown-haired girl?" Miss Finney asked. "What about her?"

"I want to tell you about the red-headed lieutenant," I said. "He came next. And I want you to tell me about Dr. Gollmer."

"Cold-leaving girl first," Miss Finney said patiently.

"Well, she got up and walked out of the café."

"Indeed," said Miss Finney. "So?"

So she didn't just get up and leave. When Madame Morelli came in she saw this girl and the woman with her at the table and she smiled at them, but she didn't get any smile back. They looked at Madame Morelli and the string of men following her, and the girl's face turned the color of the magenta ice in front of her, and the middle-aged woman's face sort of snapped tight together, and they gathered up their packages and walked out and left their ices melting on the table.

Schmitty turned to me and said, "Did you see that?"

I said, "Everybody in the place saw that."

Schmitty said, "It must be very, very pleasant *chez Morelli* of an evening, when they all meet together in friendly family union and talk over the events of the day. That was Madame Morelli's daughter."

I figured rapidly and said, "Arithmetic says I doubt that."

"Oh, well, stepdaughter," said Schmitty. "A very reserved little number, especially by contrast."

"The old job with her looked as if she had a few reservations herself," I said.

"Oh, a *very* reserved type," Schmitty said. "The girl's aunt, maiden aunt. The girl's mother's sister. Morelli's sister-in-law by first wife. Let's see, now, that makes her—I don't know what the hell that makes her to our little friend shorty-pants at the bar."

"I imagine it makes her a thorn in the flesh," I said, and Schmitty said something indecent about how there could be worse fates than to be a thorn in that particular flesh, which I guess I have now repeated, and that was that.

Miss Finney listened to me tell all this, then asked, "What are their names?"

"The girl, Jeanne. Morelli, of course. The aunt, Mademoiselle—or Madame by courtesy since she's passed *un certain âge*—Madame de St. Nicaise."

"That's a hell of a fancy name," Miss Finney commented.

"You ought to see her living up to it," I said. "I know her a little, and the girl a little too. I'll tell you about them."

"It's getting to be quite a list," Miss Finney said.

"Including Dr. Gollmer, from you," I reminded her.

She said, "I suppose you have an idea what that's all about?"

"I have a general idea. I have an idea that you'll never write up the Morelli case for the medical journals."

"That's right."

"But maybe for the criminal record."

Miss Finney said grimly, "You're on the right track, of course. But if I can work it the way I think I can, I hope I won't write it up for anything, or tell anybody about it, or do anything except—" She stopped.

"Except what?"

She shrugged, hesitated, then said, "Except straighten it out, maybe. I don't know where I am, yet, Hoop. Don't badger me. Will you tell me about the red-headed lieutenant now?"

I took a deep breath.

CHAPTER THREE

This was during the time of the North African campaign, and almost every week-end we used to get a plane load or two of service men, sometimes enlisted men but usually officers, and most usually pilots, flown down to Léopoldville for a rest. My idea of a rest isn't to fly half a continent in the bucket seats of a stripped-down DC3 and stay a day and a half and then fly back, but with these boys it always seemed to work fine.

They were certainly a nice bunch, for the most part, and they always came to Léopoldville after a very thorough briefing to the effect that they were to watch their conduct and not bust loose, that the Belgians and British in Léopold-ville would regard them as representatives of the whole American armed force and it was up to them to behave, and so on. The result was that at the Saturday night parties at the Club, toward the end of the night, there was always a circle of sober American striplings sitting around at a table looking dazed at the goings-on all around them, because these parties always tended to get pretty raucous and loose-jointed toward the end.

These boys were good at keeping watch on one another, too, and when one of them began to step out of line, the others were very adept at straightening him out. He would disappear, and either you didn't see him the rest of that evening, or when he appeared later, looking fresh-combed and clean-faced again, he would have stopped weaving, or talking too loud, or offending husbands.

I don't mean to give the impression that these boys were a bunch of Eagle Scouts or that they all looked like the starry-eyed models in the war posters. They were full of the usual fatigues and neuroses, and a lot of them came to Léopoldville hunting just one thing, and a lot of them found it there, because it was more than ordinarily available there just as it was everywhere else during the war, and as everybody knows, it was particularly available to transients surrounded by a patriotic-romantic aura. Very especially it was available to these boys, with their high average of good looks and, above all, their novelty, in an ingrown community where everybody had got so tired of everybody else's face and mannerisms and conversation that sometimes you felt as if you were involved in a kind of multiple matrimonial deadlock that had gone flat long ago.

The point in going on at some length about the virtues of these boys is that the one I am going to talk about most was a pilot who shall be called Lieutenant Malcolm since that was not his name, and who, in my books, was a pure, unadulterated, dyed-in-the-wool yard-wide son of a bitch.

He came down one week-end with ten or a dozen others, and he was one of the two we put up at our place. He was a great big red-faced orange-haired fellow maybe twenty-two years old, with an unblemished but coarse-grained skin, wiry eyebrows, and a chest and shoulders like the ones they rub down with oil to make them shine for photographs in the muscle magazines. Unfortunately he also had a big broad behind and his legs were a little too short, so that although he walked with his chin away up and his chest stuck out so far in front of him that he should have carried a small red warning flag on it in traffic, his strut had a tendency to backfire on him and turn into a plain old waddle. The other pilots called him Tiny.

These boys were always bowled over by Léopoldville when they first saw it. The inconveniences of living there, the hundreds of irritating daily precautions, the tensions and the isolation, the monotonous diet, the monotonous faces, the monotonous diversions, and all the tropical deceptions—the sudden unexplainable sickness, the persistent itching, the small but incurable running sore, the hard spot that appears on your arm or stomach or eyeball and might be a small cyst, until a filament begins working its way out of the center of it and you discover it's a guinea worm—all these equatorial treacheries which keep erupting through the Europeanized surface of life aren't apparent when you first see the place. Instead, you see the broad paved streets and the pretty women and the big clean hospital and the café terraces, and during the war when they were rationed everywhere else you saw shelf after shelf of the best whiskies in the grocery stores, and plenty of sweets and pastries (three days a week) and all the tobacco anybody could smoke. There was plenty of gasoline (no spare parts if your car broke down, and of course no more cars) and no dim-out of any kind. It was a bright little imitation of the good gay cosmopolitan life, and if you were there just for a week-end, and had come from desert fighting, it didn't make any difference at all that you could take this bright little imitation and punch your finger right through it at any point.

Tiny blew into Léopoldville ready to take it by storm, and came busting into our quarters yelling, "Lead me to it, man, lead me to it!" He made it clear immediately that he expected to get "fixed up with sump'n" and he seemed surprised that a bunch of civilians whose job was the procurement and development of strategic commodities hadn't spent a lot of their time in anticipation of his visit procuring and developing the commodity he was interested in. For about five minutes Tiny was funny, then he was just something big and noisy and in the way. We showed him his bed and told him what time supper was and then tried to get back to work in our offices, which adjoined the quarters, but all the rest of the afternoon I had the impression that we were working to an obbligato of bull-like bellowings and the crashing of furniture.

The other pilot we put up that week-end was a trim, medium-sized, nice fresh-looking boy that I just remember as Bev, short for something unfortunate like Beverly, I suppose, and he followed along in Tiny's wake, managing by sheer navigational agility to avoid being caught up in his slipstream. He looked a little embarrassed for Tiny and very much on the alert as if he were ready to step in and take hold if Tiny got altogether out of control.

Around five o'clock when we were getting ready to close up the office, Bev and Tiny came in and said thanks a lot for the invitation to supper but they thought they would go down to the ABC Hotel where the other pilots were staying, and join forces with them.

"Yeah, man!" Tiny bellowed. "Cain't waste *no* time when you need it the way I need it! Got to start lookin' *now!*"

He blew out the door. Bev followed him, and turned and gave us a half-apologetic look just before he disappeared. I said to Tommy Slattery, my boss, at the next desk, "Do you think we really ought to let something like that loose around here?"

"He won't have any luck," said Tommy, who had a profound knowledge of such things.

"He's going to disgrace us, though," I said.

"He's not our responsibility," Tommy said. "Forget it. He's an ass but we can't do anything about it."

We went over to the quarters, to the dining room, and had our usual before-dinner argument about the Old-Fashioneds, Tommy claiming it was important to dissolve the sugar in a teaspoonful of sparkling water, when it is obviously ridiculous that that little bit of sparkling water could make any difference in that much drink. We sat there drinking them

23

for a while and I had almost forgotten about Tiny when Tommy said all of a sudden, "You know, that guy's pathetic," and in a way I guess he was.

Pathetic or not pathetic, Tiny wasn't something I felt sorry for or friendly toward, that night at the party at the Club. These parties were never any good anyway, for my money. In the first place you danced to the same twenty or thirty scratched, worn-out old phonograph records every night, since you couldn't get new ones during the war, and they were piped through a beat-up loud speaker that brought out the worst in them, and when you bring out the worst in a saxophone, you've really brought out something terrible.

Even with a decent band, the parties would have been monotonous and all alike. During the first part of the evening there would be some of the genteel young ladies of the city there, always with their mothers looking hawk-eyed at the ringside, and then about midway of the evening these girls would all be taken home and put to bed under padlock. Then for the next couple of hours it would be all the brighter married set and the bachelors, with a pretty heavy concentration of effort at the bar. Then the husbands and wives who were really interested in staying married to one another would leave, and the dregs of the party would go on and on with everybody getting mixed up with everybody else. There would be maybe a couple of quarrels and there would be a lot of unbecoming letting down of hair all over the place, until finally the whole thing would grind to an end and everybody would go home frustrated and feeling like hell. The most you could hope for would be that you might get involved in some new difficulty which would complicate your life for the next week or so to the extent that for a while you could substitute a kind of excited apprehension and remorse for the standard variety of ennui. So, in many respects, it was like the usual country club party in American suburbia, except that if you just had to go somewhere Saturday night, there wasn't anyplace else to go. There was the hotel, and the terrace there was pleasant, but it closed at midnight and also it was public, and what I am talking about is the elite, not the *hoi polloi.*

I put off going to the club this night as long as possible, by going to the movie first. The film industry's export policy to the Congo seems to be to start at the bottom and make every effort to keep from working up. This one was Anna Neagle in *Irene,* which I remembered from years back as the worst movie I had ever seen, and it still held the record. It was comforting in a way because I could sit there and reflect that there were people more unfortunate than I, namely Miss Neagle and anybody else who had got involved in that quicksand, while all I had to do was sit in an uncomfortable chair and watch them struggle. Then when it was over, I made the rounds of the café terraces, hoping as I always did that the Hausa men, the vendors of curios who lined up and spread out their wares on the pavement, might have something better than the badly cured leather and routine ebony elephants which were their stock in trade. I found a little ivory pig that wasn't too bad. I didn't see Tiny or Bev or any of their friends at any of the cafés so I supposed they were already at the Club. Finally I couldn't find any other way to kill time so I went there myself.

The party was entering its tertiary stage, and Tiny was there, all right. He was dancing with Liliane Morelli and there wasn't anything casual about it. He was making the most obvious kind of direct frontal attack in full force. Everybody was watching them, and anybody but Liliane would have found some way to get away from him. There was something in his attitude that said, "Look at me, folks"; he seemed to me to be less fascinated with Liliane than with the idea that Lieutenant Tiny Malcolm was putting on quite a show and making quite a conquest for one and all to see. The way he danced around and the way he concentrated on

25

Liliane, never looking away from her, and talking a blue streak all the time and grinning, and sometimes whispering in her ear—the way he did all this, he was asking you every minute to notice that this American pilot was quite a man and that he was certainly giving Madame Morelli the business. Now and then he would stop talking long enough to get cheek to cheek, then he would close his eyes and look dreamy and try some fancy step or other.

I must say for Liliane that even if she didn't have the sense to get away from him, she was only allowing herself to be propelled around the floor, rather than co-operating one hundred per cent. When Tiny lunged or whirled or dipped, she managed to take the edge off his excesses by resisting a little bit, but it was still a gruesome spectacle. He was making her look big and awkward, but she didn't look bothered or embarrassed, and she listened to him with steady interest, as if she enjoyed the attention, and I guess she did, because that was what she loved more than anything in the world, attention.

Bev was dancing too, and when I caught his eye he gave me a quick smile and jerked his head in the direction of Tiny as if to say that it was pretty funny but everything was under control. The rest of their bunch was either dancing or sitting at their big table, and it was as quiet a night as I had ever seen at the Club, although there was the usual ruckus at the bar.

Morelli wasn't there, at the bar or outside on the veranda or anywhere. But then he seldom was. Sometimes he would bring Liliane, then disappear early while she stayed on, or sometimes she would tag along with a party of two or three couples, maybe with an escort or maybe not. That wasn't too unusual around town, but with Liliane it was a regular thing.

I fooled around outside, where it was cooler and I wouldn't

have to see Tiny. I talked to people I knew, for maybe half an hour or forty-five minutes. Then I decided I couldn't stand the sound of the music any longer so I said good night to a couple of people and went to get the car. That night I had the discouraged old Dodge we rented at the office, and when I went to look for it in the Club's parking lot, it was gone. I hadn't locked it because I didn't want to carry the keys around, and anyway you didn't bother to lock your car because the idea of a car theft in Léopoldville was ridiculous. There were so few cars that any one of them could be spotted quickly, and there wasn't anywhere to drive a stolen car after you had it. I knew right away what had happened.

I went over to the table where a couple of the pilots were sitting and asked them if they knew where Tiny was. I noticed that Bev was still out there dancing.

The pilots said Tiny had just that minute left, with the job he had been dancing with. They looked surprised and said he had gone in my car, and that he had said it was all right with me.

"It's all right," I said. "I just wanted to be sure."

I decided to let Bev do his own worrying when he noticed Tiny was gone, and went out and found a taxi and went home.

It was around two that morning, about the time the parties at the Club usually broke up, when I heard a car, not ours, drive up, and then drive away. I was in bed, with the light out, but not asleep, and in a couple of minutes I heard somebody walking quietly outside my room. The outside door was open but the screen was latched; a vague silhouette appeared back of the screen, and I recognized Bev, even before he spoke. He tapped on the screen with one finger and whispered, "You awake?" If there was any real trouble, anything I could do anything about, I knew Bev would wake me, but if there wasn't anything to do, I didn't even want to talk about it. I just lay there in the dark, watching Bev while

27

he watched me, and after a moment he went away, and I heard the door to the room he and Tiny shared open and close.

Later I woke up to the sound of our car going into the garage, and saw by my bedside clock that it was four o'clock. I heard Tiny blundering along in the dark and going into his and Bev's room. Immediately there was a murmur of voices. For a minute they raised quickly, although I couldn't catch the words, then they shushed again. I was wide awake, and good and curious, and getting mad when I thought about Tiny, so I got up and put on a robe and went to their room.

Bev was standing there in his skivvy shorts. He had a neat, tight-muscled little body that contrasted with Tiny's big lumpy-looking one, as Tiny sat there on the edge of the bed, in his stocking feet, fumbling soggily at his shirt buttons. Bev was tight-lipped and flushed, standing there glaring down at Tiny, but Tiny was looking down and mumbling and breathing heavily, in a hang-dog kind of way.

They both looked up as I came in, but then Tiny dropped his eyes again. Bev said to me, "I'm sorry we woke you up. And I'm sorry about the car too. I was just telling Tiny."

"Don't worry about the car," I said. I decided Tiny wasn't drunk in spite of his soggy look. And whatever had happened, I decided that Tiny hadn't had a very good time. I said to Bev, "Do you need anything—or anything?"

"We're all right," Bev said. "I haven't checked on the car."

Tiny mumbled, "Goddam car's all right." He pulled his shirt off at last, then pulled his skivvy shirt over his head, revealing a pinkish torso as big and meaty as something you'd expect to find in packer's storage, with some excelsior-like matting spread across the chest.

"I didn't come to check on the car," I said.

There was one of those blank pauses, nobody doing or saying anything, and I knew that Bev was holding himself in, ready to light into Tiny again as soon as I left. I said, "Well —if you don't need anything, I'll go back to bed. See you in the morning."

I started to the door, but just as I reached it, Tiny called out, "Hey!"

I turned, and Tiny was still sitting there like a lump, but he had raised his head and he said to me, in a forced voice, "You see that piece I was dancing with?"

"I saw you dancing with Madame Morelli," I said.

"That was a piece," Tiny said. "Look here," he said, and he glared at me as if I had denied something he had said. One hand doubled into a fist and he pounded the bed gently with it alongside his thigh. "Look here," he said, still glaring at me, "I *got* that piece tonight. I *got* it, see?"

There wasn't anything to say. I said, "You did?"

"You damn right. And another thing," Tiny said, in a strangled voice, "another thing, I want you to know—" He took a deep breath, but when he spoke again his voice was more choked than ever. "I want you to know," he managed to say, "it was *lousy*. Was it *ever* lousy." He leaned forward at me and his voice rose and he said as loud as he could, "*I got it the way I said I would, and it was lousy.*"

Then I saw the crazy fool was going to cry if I didn't go, so I turned back to the door and stepped through and closed it behind me.

I went back to my room and lit a cigarette and lay on the bed smoking it. But I didn't put down the mosquito net, or turn out the lamp, or latch the screen door, because I knew I was going to have a visit from Bev before long.

He turned up before the cigarette was finished, in pants and shirt and slippers now. He tapped at the door and came on in. He stood there looking uncertain and hesitant. I said hello, and sat up on the bed and pointed to a chair, but Bev shook his head and remained standing. He swallowed, and said, "I'm sorry about all this."

"Never mind. It really doesn't make any difference about the car, and we'll forget the rest."

"About what he just said, though."

"Yes, I know. That stank, all right."

Bev hesitated again, for a long minute, then said, "About that lady." He had avoided "woman" and "girl," but he said "lady" a little uncertainly. "I don't know her or anything," he said, "but I know Tiny."

He paused so long that finally I said, "What's on your mind?"

He blurted, "He didn't get it, that's all. I know Tiny, and I don't know whether you know this—lady, or not, but I know Tiny, and I think I ought to tell you, I bet he didn't get it the way he said he did."

"I had an idea he didn't, myself," I said. "Sit down. Tell me about it. What did he say?"

Bev took a creaky rattan chair and looked more at ease. "He didn't tell me anything he didn't tell you," he said. "Tiny isn't so bad; you just have to know how to take him. He acted like a stinker—"

"He sure did."

"—but you know how it is with some of them, they can't get it no matter how hard they try."

"He tries *too* hard," I said. I also felt like saying that Tiny was less interested in getting it than in having people think he was getting it, but I held that one in.

"I guess he does," Bev said. "But about tonight. If he *had* managed to get something, he'd have been blowing all over the place about how wonderful it was. But the way he said how lousy it was, that just means he didn't even get to first base, that's all."

All of a sudden I had a picture of the whole thing—the car parked at the roadside, probably a kiss or two, then Tiny's awkward lunge, the hot, sticky, absurd struggle in the cramped space, Liliane straining away from the bristly meat of Tiny's foraging mouth, the pawing, the pushing away, and always Tiny's awkward, impotent, floundering simulation of the lust he wanted to feel, as it ebbed away before Liliane's resistance. The male humiliation, the embarrassing ride home, the quick, relieved good night between two strangers.

I said to Bev, "But where's he been all this time?"

He said, "Probably parked somewhere, just sitting the time out."

"No doubt. Well, forget it, Bev. As a matter of fact, I don't know Madame Morelli except by sight."

But Bev still looked worried. "That's good," he said, "but it isn't only that. You see, if Tiny got a chance to say that to anyone else, he said it. There's no telling who he's said it to."

"We'll just have to hope not," I said. "Do you want a drink or anything, Bev?"

"No, thanks. I don't think so." He rose to leave.

"There's an icebox, if you're hungry."

"You haven't got a glass of milk?" he asked, as he might have asked if I had a chalice of ambrosia.

"Just Klim," I said—powdered milk that you stirred up with water.

His face fell. "We have that at the base," he said. "Well, I'll go. I'm sorry about all this, really."

I said, "Sure there isn't anything I can offer you?"

"Not a thing. Good night."

"Good night, Bev. See you at breakfast."

But Bev and Tiny's room was empty at breakfast time next morning, and Bev had left a note for me: "So long, Tolliver, many thanks, and I'm glad we got that business straightened out last night."

It might have been straightened out for me, but all over Léopoldville, from then on, there were a lot of people who would tell you all about Liliane Morelli and the red-headed American lieutenant.

Miss Finney listened to the whole story of Tiny almost

without comment. When I had finished, she sat there saying nothing, scowling across the river, which was disappearing rapidly into the approaching dark. The lights were coming on in Brazzaville on the other side. Miss Finney's sun helmet was in her lap, and she drummed lightly on its corky surface with her finger tips, a sort of *tap-tap*-atappatappa-tap, in a native rhythm. I sat and waited, glad enough for a little rest from talking.

Suddenly Miss Finney terminated the drumming with a couple of strong decisive slaps with the palm of her hand and said, "Let's go. Emily hasn't got enough sense to go get something to eat if I don't lead her to it. You're not tied up for dinner, are you?"

I started backing the car out of the overlook and said, "No, I'm not. We might go to the Petit-Pont"—a very good little restaurant just outside town.

"Good."

She hardly spoke on the way back to the hotel, except once when she said, "I don't suppose it occurred to you to try to *do* anything about that Tiny business, did it?"

"What could I do?" I asked. "Take an ad in the *Voix d'Afrique?* Something to whom it may concern, like *In the opinion of the undersigned, in spite of appearances and statements to the contrary, Madame Liliane Morelli of this city did not accede to the desires of the American lieutenant, the way they're saying all over town she did, in case you haven't heard the gossip.* Something like that?"

Miss Finney smiled and said, "I know, but for instance if anybody said anything to you—Schmitty or somebody, for instance."

"Then of course I always said I doubted it. But that's all. I didn't know anything one way or another, when you come down to it. I felt a certain way about Tiny that made me doubt it, the way everybody else in town felt a certain way about Liliane Morelli that made them believe it. In any case, she didn't mean anything to me one way or another—then."

Miss Finney cocked an eye at me, and said, "Then?" but I wasn't finished. I went on, "And anyway, try sometime taking a couple of rumors and dropping them in this town or any other community where everybody is under everybody else's nose. Drop in a rumor that so-and-so stepped out of line, and drop in another saying that on the contrary so-and-so never has stepped out of line at all. Give them an even start and see which one beats out the other one. Virtue makes awful poor fodder for gossip."

Miss Finney was looking at me hard, but I had a feeling that I was fading away before her eyes. Her face was taking on that abstracted look that always meant that the set of the random ideas and odds and ends of circumstance that she kept stored up inside her head for ultimate use had suddenly received the catalytic she had been keeping them ready for, and had begun crystallizing into a vision of heads falling. I knew what would happen: in a minute she would be all sweet innocence, because she would be covering up some typical scheme of deviltry that you couldn't get her to say a word about, come hell or high water, until she was ready to. And sure enough, after a few seconds she turned her head away and fanned her face a few times with one big hand, and said in a perfectly meaningless tea-party voice, "Goodness, it's been *hot*, hasn't it!"

It had been hot. It had been hot in Léopoldville for many years now, and would continue tó be hot for many years to come. "*That*," I said to Miss Finney, "is the silliest goddam remark I ever heard a bright woman make."

Miss Finney looked at me with raised eyebrows and said in accents of pained gentility, "Hoopie *dear!*"

I let it go at that, and we rode along in silence to the hotel to get Emily, but I had a little bit the feeling that I was sitting next to a time-bomb and I hadn't any idea what time it was set for.

CHAPTER FOUR

Dr. Gollmer was in his middle fifties. He was a very tall man—around six-two, I'd say, and that made him the tallest man in Léopoldville, where, if people tended to run over size, they did it in width rather than length. The most noticeable thing about Dr. Gollmer's general build was the prominence of his bones. He was not a thin man—spare-fleshed, you might say, but not thin—and yet you were always aware of these bones, which were of great size. Particularly, his joints were big and heavy, and gave the impression that they were less flexible than other people's, as if formed on a simpler pattern, a more primitive one, or made of a substance more coarse-grained than bone, so that they had had to be more simply executed. As a result, his movements were somewhat slow and stiff, deliberate, although not exactly awkward. He played the violin, and he was pretty good. I imagine that without the primary difficulty of his hand-type, for his hands were not only as long and narrow as the rest of him but also as broad-boned, he would have been very good. The joints of his fingers had the same quality as the rest of his body, the quality of limited flexibility.

But if his body suggested inflexibility, Dr. Gollmer was generally credited with the most flexible set of morals in town, so flexible that although he had come to be something like the town's official bohemian—he occupied a sort of spiritual Left Bank all by himself—he had a superb tolerance for the conventionality of other people's lives. If that was the kind of life they were fools enough to lead by choice, he seemed to say, let them lead it.

Dr. Gollmer had a long, narrow, hard-fleshed face in which the nose had at some time been flattened and pushed slightly to the left. It was typical of the impression he made that although I never heard anything about how he got his nose broken, I always took it for granted that it was broken in some kind of disreputable brawl. His eyelids were heavy, and they supported a coarse growth of lashes; his mouth was wide, irregular, and firm. I found his face altogether a good one, but like other Left-Bankers, Dr. Gollmer was always preoccupied with the growing of hair on it. His beard had the coarseness of a heavy fiber brush, irregularly bristled in red, black, gray, and white. These bristles had the same simplified and oversize quality as his bones, so that you could sit across a table from him and be aware of any individual bristle —red, black, gray, or white—as a bristle of a certain shape and size, projecting itself out of its individual follicle with great independence and definition. But Dr. Gollmer never stuck very long to any one arrangement of these bristles. Sometimes he would be growing a mustache, sometimes a beard, and sometimes long sideburns, but none of these ever got very far beyond the preliminary stubbly stage.

When I first came to Léopoldville, Dr. Gollmer was still respectable enough to be received almost anywhere, although even then, at the very best houses, he was asked only to the largest parties. By the time I had left Léopoldville and returned for my second stay there, Dr. Gollmer had indulged his moral flexibility to such an extent that the good people he so easily forgave had found it impossible to forgive him, and he had become the next thing to a pariah.

But at this time, the early stage of the game, he was received even by Madame de St. Nicaise, Morelli's sister-in-law by his first wife, and the gentility of Madame de St. Nicaise was absolutely closed to any question whatsoever. She spent her life keeping it so. This was the time of the Great Stringed Instrument Schism, with Dr. Gollmer and

Madame de St. Nicaise as protagonists, which tore artistic Léopoldville stem to stern, and had more connection with the death of Liliane Morelli than anyone could have foreseen— or, for that matter, ever discerned at all, even by hindsight.

The Fine Arts in Léopoldville, as in most places, were on the town. There is a very good little museum of native arts, with some fine pieces, although all the very best had been sent to Brussels, for the museum there. When Goering had all these pieces packed up and sent to Germany, a lot of people in Léopoldville who had always thought of native art as nothing more than a local novelty to be patronized by tourists and eccentrics began to look at it with a new interest, because obviously if Goering wanted it, along with the Ghent altarpiece and, for that matter, all of Belgium itself, then it must be better than they had thought.

The Léopoldville museum was run by a society called *Les Amis de l'Art Indigène du Congo Belge* and for a while they put out a magazine called *Brousse*, which means "bush," a word meaning the jungle in particular but the less civilized portions of the Congo in general. It was an excellent little magazine and Dr. Gollmer used to write for it. Even while he was still an acceptable member of the social community, he wasn't too good a doctor to have for anything like an extended illness, because whenever he felt like it and could scrape together enough money for it, he would kite off to Popokabaka to do another article on the arts of the Batshiok. These Batshiok are good-looking people and among the most talented tribes in the Congo, the only ones with a lyrical love poetry, for instance, and with one of the most highly developed styles of native sculpture. They have a formalized ballet, performed once a year on the occasion of the circumcision and acceptance into the tribe of the boys who have reached puberty, and this ballet is supposed to be the finest dance in Central Africa except for the royal dance of the

Watusi, which everybody who knows Africa at all knows from movies of it.

From time to time you would hear of Dr. Gollmer that he was off with his Batshiok again, and if he left a patient in the final stages of pregnancy, he obviously felt that the birth of one white baby was of less importance than the investigation of a fine culture which was disappearing by the minute under the white man's vulgarization. On the occasions of these trips, while he was still in the comparative good graces of the community, there would be a certain coy arching of eyebrows to indicate that our dear Dr. Gollmer was indulging his personal taste for the bizarre along with his hobby of research in native arts; after his fall into disfavor you would hear exactly the same thing said, but in tones of opprobrium. But whatever Dr. Gollmer did in the villages, and certainly there was something in his mien which indicated that he wouldn't hesitate to satisfy any outlandish curiosity he might feel, he always returned with something worth rescuing—some poems or songs, which he would translate for *Brousse*, a transcription of a melody, or a notation of a drum rhythm, and once some fuzzy snapshots of the ballet, which professional anthropologists had never managed to photograph at all.

He would always bring back another really good example or two of the constantly diminishing store of masks and fetishes used in the ceremonies. He would sell some of these, if he needed money too badly, but no money could buy the best ones from him. In his house, a small decaying structure nearly consumed by vines and bushes, the walls bristled with spears, knives, and arrows; dripped with bead necklaces twisted into ropes as thick as your arm and with strings of leopard teeth; stared at you with the eyes of bush-devil masks; and everywhere, on tables and shelves and window sills, there were figures carved of wood or ivory, or fabricated of raffia and feathers, some of them with little bits of mirror inlaid for eyes, some with real human hair, many with human teeth inserted higgledy-piggledy in their mouths, some stained with the blood and excrement which invested them with magical powers, and here and there one of such repose and serenity that it stood clean and unaffected by the enveloping dark.

That was the Dr. Gollmer of my first year in Léopold-ville. Of all the people connected with the Morelli affair, he was the one who changed most from that time until the death of Liliane Morelli. During that first year, even, you could see him begin going downhill after his quarrel with Madame de St. Nicaise. During the time I was away, in the service, I used to hear from Schmitty, and he wrote me all about the scandal involving Dr. Gollmer and Liliane, which brought Dr. Gollmer further discredit. By the time I came back to Léopoldville, Dr. Gollmer looked ten years older, and was well on his way to becoming the town bum. He had very few patients, he owed small sums of money to everybody, and he frequently smelled of whisky before noon.

I liked Dr. Gollmer—taking him on faith, since I had never done much more than exchange greetings with him at parties—and I was glad when he got his first real break in a long time. A small and faintly crack-brained expedition of French and American anthropologists, technicians, and dab-blers came over on a grant from some foundation or other to make movies of native dances and records of native music. They were working out of Brazzaville, across the river, up into various parts of French Equatorial Africa, and they picked up Dr. Gollmer to serve as translator and general liaison man in the villages. He spent six months with this bunch, and came back with enough cash to square away most of his debts. He put out his shingle in earnest, determined to re-establish himself as a respectable doctor.

In a funny kind of way, Dr. Gollmer seemed to have got himself married and settled down. His wife was a pair of young women named Mademoiselle Lala and Mademoiselle

Baba; they seemed to serve a secondary function as children. The three of them—Dr. Gollmer, Mademoiselle Lala, and Mademoiselle Baba—came back to his little house, chopped away enough vines to get into the front door, and set up a *ménage à trois*.

Mademoiselle Lala and Mademoiselle Baba were in their very early twenties, no more than that. They were very much of a size, both short, around five-three, and they both smiled all the time, in a sweet, unaware kind of way. Beyond the fact that both of them traveled under French passports, no one ever learned anything about their antecedents. Lala was Lala's real name, but Baba was a name which attached itself to Baba because Lala and Baba obviously had to have names which paired closely enough to suggest their virtual identity with one another, and because Baba herself suggested the sweet plump bready cake of that name. Baba was a natural brunette, with the short legs, chunky breasts, wide shoulders, and apple cheeks of the peasant of the south of France.

Lala on the other hand was an unnatural blonde. Her hair was coarse, and looked as if it would have been kinky if it had not been kept straightened. It was the hot tarnished brassy color of very black hair which has been crudely bleached, and although her eyes were gray, they had the unnatural look of light eyes in a mulatto, for her skin was the creamy dark beige of a magnolia turned brown—really a beautiful skin. Finally, she had suspiciously long feet with heels projecting sharply back behind the ankle, and suspiciously high, tight-knotted little calves on her skimpy shanks. She had some story or other about an Egyptian father and an Italian mother.

You seldom saw Lala and Baba without Dr. Gollmer. The girls had tidied him up considerably, and they themselves were always neat and clean in cheap sleazy dresses, made of bad imitation silk, with hemlines just above their knees no matter what the fashion was. They were decked with a whole dime-store counterful of bracelets, rings, earrings, necklaces, and pins, set with green and red and yellow and blue glass stones. When they were not with Dr. Gollmer they were together, always extremely cheerful, always open and friendly, but never speaking to anybody, since nobody under any circumstances spoke to them except in stores across counters. They seemed not to resent this; they seemed not to resent anything or to worry about anything, and they always seemed to me the most contented-looking pair I had ever run across in those parts. When the three of them walked down the street, Lala would be hooked on one of Dr. Gollmer's arms and Baba on the other. When the girls walked together, they went hand in hand, like children. There was something sweet and even pastoral about the whole business. I have always been able to imagine a fireplace in Dr. Gollmer's house, with Dr. Gollmer sitting in front of it in pajamas and bathrobe, and Lala and Baba symmetrically disposed on low footstools at either side of him, their heads resting on the arms of his chair, and the firelight glinting on the green, red, yellow, and blue glass stones of the knick-knack jewelry their dear protector had given them.

Mary Finney, of course, already knew a lot about Dr. Gollmer. There are legends in the Congo, which for all I know may be absolutely true, about news traveling from one end of the place to the other by drum more quickly than by telegraph. Whatever it was that Mary Finney used as the equivalent of communication by drum, she knew all there was to know about every doctor in the Congo, whether she had ever actually corresponded with him, or been called into consultation with him, or not. So there wasn't anything I could tell her about Dr. Gollmer's general character or the general pattern of his career, but she had never heard of the Great

Stringed Instrument Schism, which had been social rather than medical in inception.

"This is absolutely beside the point," I told her. "There's no reason in telling you this, it's just something that happened that was awfully funny at the time, but it couldn't possibly have anything to do with what you're interested in."

"Maybe not," Miss Finney said, "and maybe so. You never can tell. But I do know that I'd rather you wasted your time telling it to me than that I wasted mine trying to figure what I'm trying to figure, without knowing something that it *might* tell me."

"What might it tell you?" I asked.

"Hell's—own—fire," Miss Finney said patiently. "How do I know what it'll tell me? Maybe nothing. Maybe a lot. I tell you I've just got to get everything you can give me. I'll pick and choose the pieces that might mean something. All you have to do is talk. The less you try to think, the better." She said all this in the particular way she had of somehow speaking crossly, but letting you know that if she wasn't really fond of you she wouldn't be acting cross at all.

We had been waiting at the hotel for Emily Collins, so that all of us could go to the Petit-Pont for dinner, and now Emily came out all set to take off. Miss Collins weighed easily a hundred pounds and always gave the impression of being freshly dusted with talcum and turned out in starched dimity, and frequently when I think I am thinking of her I discover that I am not really thinking of her at all, but of Lillian Gish in *The Birth of a Nation*. As a pure matter of fact, I can remember that on this evening she was wearing on her head the companion to Miss Finney's sun helmet, and on the little contraption that served her for a body she was wearing the curious sacklike garment which one Léopold-ville dressmaker had once asked the privilege of examining sometime when Miss Collins didn't have it on, because she simply could not figure out how several pieces of cloth which had presumably been cut and sewn together by something other than chance could possibly have resulted in anything that looked so meaningless. Miss Finney often said that in their relationship as missionaries she represented the flesh and the devil while Emily ran the soul and hymn department, and certainly Emily's costume symbolized complete renunciation of the body, for it denied that what was tied up inside it was anything other than a small fragile bundle of twigs. I was extremely fond of Emily, and so was Miss Finney.

She came forward to us now, walking quite straight, I am certain, but giving the impression of creeping sidewise with the particular air of apologetic self-effacement which was her very own.

"Hello, dear Hoopie," she said, and timidly extended to me the small, ineffectual-looking hand in which I had once, with my own eyes, seen her grasp a forty-five and plug a difficult customer who at that moment had been giving Miss Finney a lot of trouble. It is true that Emily fainted immediately after, but it is on record that she plugged him, all the same.

I took her hand, and she withdrew it quickly. She ducked what I had intended to be a peck on the cheek, with an agility which suggested more practice at that kind of thing than she could possibly have had. She came out of the maneuver a little flustered, pulled inconclusively a couple of times at her garment as if to straighten it, and said, "Let's eat."

We started out to the car, and Miss Finney said, "Emily, I was just telling Hoopie about Dr. Gollmer," which, since we hadn't mentioned Dr. Gollmer's name for some time, I took to be a cue that any further talk from me was out, until we got rid of Emily.

"Dr. *Goll*mer," breathed Emily. "Oh, *dear.*"

"Emily doesn't like Dr. Gollmer," Miss Finney said. "She thinks he is a horrid man."

"Oh, indeed I *do*," said Emily, and then with more spirit, "and indeed he *is*. Anybody can tell that. Just to look at him."

Miss Finney said, "He suggests to Emily an excessive indulgence in the pleasures of the bed and the bottle."

"I never said that," said Emily.

"Oh yes you did, but you didn't admit they were pleasures," said Miss Finney, so smugly that I had a suspicion she had been amusing herself, as she frequently did, by seeing if she could manipulate the conversation around to the point where she could get somebody to say something in the exact words she wanted them to say it in.

I said, "You're right, Emmy, he looks terrible," because although he had spruced up a little, I remembered how vigorous he had been when I first knew him, and how broken he looked now.

"He's taking the Morelli thing very hard," Miss Finney said. We had got downstairs now, and to the car. We climbed in, all three in the front seat because Emily took up no more room than a sack of groceries, and didn't generate much more in the way of body heat. Miss Finney said, "I'll tell you about that, Hoop. Know anything about blackwater fever?"

What I knew about blackwater fever was that you usually died from it, and that everybody was always saying "Be sure to take your quinine," the idea being that if you got malaria and then had to take the big doses of quinine they gave you in treatment of it, the malaria might turn into blackwater if you hadn't already accustomed your system to the quinine by taking the five or ten grains a day which were standard. But you heard all kinds of things—for instance, after we had taken our quinine for months in the pill form they sold to us in the Congo, we heard somewhere that you had to mash them up, because the pills were so hard they went right through you, otherwise. And a lot of people took quinine all the time and got malaria, and a lot claimed they never took it at all, and never got anything at all, and so forth and so on in every possible combination. And once for five weeks I had taken Tommy Slattery's bicarbonate-of-soda tablets every day thinking they were the quinine tablets that looked just the same and came from the same place in the same kind of box, labeled with the very unlovely name of the drug chain, *Compagnie Pharmaceutique du Congo—Cophaco*. I said all this to Miss Finney.

She said, "Well, I wouldn't say you had an exhaustive knowledge of blackwater, but you've got the popular essentials down. You could look it up in a book and learn something. For the moment I'll tell you that for reasons sufficient unto myself I talked to Gollmer yesterday and asked him to outline the treatment he gave Liliane—quinine dosage and so on—when she came down with malaria. He did it all according to routine procedure, and according to routine procedure there isn't any reason in the world why it should have turned into blackwater."

"Does that have to mean anything?" I asked.

"It doesn't *have* to," Miss Finney said. "On the other hand, it easily could. But this has hit him awfully hard. He did hope for a comeback, although considering the way people feel about these two girls of his—"

"Mademoiselle Lala and Mademoiselle Baba," I said.

"Yeah," said Miss Finney. She grinned. "That old goat," she said. "Well, what with all this Lalababa stuff and the fact that you can see he's turning into an old drunk and what with one thing and another, I guess you know he's really been on the rocks, and when he was called in by the Morellis he felt he was really ready for a comeback."

"I can't understand how they happened to call him in,"

I said. "He hasn't had a respectable patient for a long time."

"Or a paying one either," Miss Finney said. "He told me the reason they called him in was that Liliane insisted on having him."

"*Liliane* did?"

"So he says. It's surprising, but you're consternated. Why?"

"If Liliane really called him in, I'd say it was a pretty generous gesture, that's all."

"Why?"

"Something he did to her, that's all," I said, remembering Emily was listening. "This is your story. Go ahead."

"That's all there is to it," Miss Finney said. "He seems to have diagnosed the case properly, he seems to have treated it properly, as malaria, but on the other hand he certainly has lost his patient, which, for him, means final curtain as a doctor. It's one too many, and especially it's one too prominent."

"What does he expect you to do about it?" I asked.

"As a matter of fact he seems a little uncertain as to whether he wants me to do anything at all about it. A well-wisher of his came to me, and—"

"I didn't know he had any well-wishers any more. Except maybe me."

"You?" Miss Finney asked. "How come you?"

"I don't know—no particular reason except that I've always liked him without knowing him, really—always felt he had an odd kind of honesty that explains a lot of the things people object to in him."

Miss Finney looked at me with the combination of calculation and beneficence that was one of her typical expressions when she was pleased, and said, "You're a mass of flaws and shortcomings, Hoopie, but you've got some very endearing virtues. I'm glad you feel that quality in old Gollmer. I feel it too, or I wouldn't be fooling with this case. I'm supposed to issue some kind of statement. People are talking about malpractice, at worst, or just plain incompetence, at best. I'm supposed to issue this statement saying that Gollmer made a correct diagnosis and gave the correct treatment and that in my opinion nobody could have done anything more."

"And coming from Mary Finney, that does Gollmer a lot of good," I said.

"Sure," Miss Finney said, matter-of-factly.

"And who's this well-wisher?"

Miss Finney ignored the question so ostentatiously that I asked another. "Can you do it for him?" I asked.

"How can I? I didn't see the patient. He had remarkably complete records, though. Madame de St. Nicaise ran a very orderly establishment for Madame Morelli, whether she liked her or not. Daily records of everybody's quinine dosage for years past, even including guests, for goodness' sake. Gollmer had all the temperature graphs and records of medication in good order. I wouldn't be able to say a thing except that from what he told me and showed me everything seems all right except that it didn't work. And according to him, Liliane was strong as a horse, hadn't been sick a day since she came to the Congo. And that's a record for any woman. She should have weathered this."

"I can't imagine her sick, much less dead. Is that all you know?"

"The essentials."

"Then why are you doing all this?"

Miss Finney hesitated for a long time, then said uncomfortably, "I'm suspicious."

"What makes you suspicious? If that's all you know."

"Things you've told me, mostly," she said. "When I first mentioned it to you, I was shooting in the dark. Now I'm shooting *at* something."

"You wouldn't want to go so far as to say at some*body*, would you?" I asked.

At this point Emily gave one of her small apologetic coughs and said, "I sincerely trust, Mary, that you are not pointing the finger of suspicion at Madame de St. Nicaise."

We had got to the Petit-Pont, but Miss Finney said, "Wait a minute, Hoop, don't get out, we're going to sit right here and listen to this." She turned full to her partner and said, "Emily Collins, do you know this Nicaise woman?"

"Indeed I do," said Emily.

"Well for *Pete's* sake," Miss Finney said. "Right in my own back yard. How come?"

"I was with Madame de St. Nicaise this afternoon," said Emily, in a virtuous tone which seemed to add, "while you and Hoopie were sitting around in bars. And I may say that I found her completely charming."

"Oh, you may?" said Miss Finney. "And may I ask why you were with her?"

"Madame de St. Nicaise is chairlady of the *Société des Dames Belgiques pour—*" Emily took a deep preparatory breath and shifted gear into English—"The Belgian Ladies' Society for the Encouragement of Christian Music Among the Congo Natives. The Society is giving us fifty new hymnals *and*," she said, looking as smug as Mary Finney had ever looked, although I had never before seen Emily look even faintly pleased with herself, "*and* a portable foot-pump-organ."

Miss Finney looked stunned. She said, "Well, for crying out loud, pump-organs, and me needing hypodermics the way I do." Then she beamed and said, "Little Emily, and Madame de St. Nicaise. Who'd have thought it?" She contemplated Emily with pleasure, and said, "Hot dog!" She followed this with, "Whaddayaknow," and then, still grinning, she wound up her soliloquy: "Emily Collins, I can *use* you," she said.

All during dinner she kept on grinning, and now and then she would shake her head in wonder and delight, and although

I would have been feeling very uncomfortable indeed if I had been in Emily's position, indeed I would, Emily seemed happy and content, and pecked away at her food so steadily that she downed many an ounce before we took her home and put her to bed, and Miss Finney and I went automobile riding again so that I could tell her about the Great Stringed Instrument Schism for whatever it might be worth to her as part of the rat's nest of information which she kept stored away inside her head for future refinement and selection.

CHAPTER FIVE

What they say about politics and bedfellows is true enough, but the strangeness of these combinations is as nothing compared with the strangeness of the heads that find themselves on the same pillow because of art. Nothing else in this world, except maybe a mutual love of fishing, which they didn't happen to share, could have produced a union between Madame de St. Nicaise and Dr. Gollmer. And even this union through art was effected with difficulty and preserved, as long as it lasted, in pain.

On the face of it you wouldn't have said they could get together even on art. Dr. Gollmer was a member of the Friends of Native Art and a contributor to *Brousse*, and it was typical of Madame de St. Nicaise that she should be involved in something for the Encouragement of Christian Music Among the Congo Natives, because she was one of those unwilling inhabitants of the Congo who look on anything native as anathema. *Ces indigènes*, these natives, is for them a term of contempt and revulsion, and anything having to do with native art, native culture, native anything, is something to be destroyed if possible, or hidden as second best, or ignored if you can't do any better, and finally simply tolerated if it is something you can't get along without, like native servants.

But Dr. Gollmer played the violin and Madame de St. Nicaise played the cello, and they were joined in quadruple musical alliance with the two other members of the Léopold String Quartet, which gave two concerts a year.

I went into the Consulate one morning, not long after Schmitty and I had sat at the café and I had been left cold by Jeanne Morelli, and when I came in, I thought Schmitty said, "Hello, chum."

"Chum yourself, bud."

"I didn't say *chum*," Schmitty said. "I said chump." He reached into his desk drawer and pulled out a small packet of pasteboard slips held together by a rubber band. He pulled the top one off the bunch and held it out to me, and when I didn't take it he laid it down on the desk in front of me.

"Fifty francs," he said. That was around a dollar seventy-five.

"You go to hell," I suggested.

"Not this time," Schmitty said. "This time I've got you by where you can't pull away. This is the local equivalent of the ticket to the Policemen's Ball. Fifty francs."

I looked at the pasteboard, which was a ticket for a concert by something called the Léopold String Quartet, proceeds to go to the benefit of Belgian refugees. The only Belgian refugees I knew were those in Léopoldville who had got out by way of London with generous wads of dough and were now happily selling their Congo copper and tin and everything else as fast as they could pull it out of the ground, and I said to Schmitty that unless there was another brand of Belgian refugee somewhere who needed my fifty francs worse than I did, no tickee.

"No tickee my foot," Schmitty said. "Into every life some rain must fall. This is yours for today. Matter of foreign policy. You wouldn't undo all the State Department's work for a lousy fifty francs, would you?" He held out his hand and rubbed the finger tips together. "Give," he said. I gave.

"As a matter of fact," Schmitty said, after we had gone out and got settled over morning coffee at the Equatoriale, "the Quartet isn't so bad. You remember that old biddy we

50

saw here the other day? The one that stalked out when Madame Stuff walked in? Wait'll you see her lovin' up that bull fiddle.''

It wasn't a bull fiddle Madame de St. Nicaise played, it was a cello, as I've said, but when you saw her playing it, you understood why Schmitty, who had an indecent turn of mind whenever possible, spoke in amorous metaphor. Madame de St. Nicaise was not a tall woman, and if cellos come in different sizes, this must have been an awfully large one. Female cellists are always in a spot at a concert; there's always that awkward moment when they sit down and assume the ungainly attitude in preparation for accommodating the instrument. Once they get going, all's well, and they are part of the instrument, if they're really good; the big instrument and the person playing it are part and parcel of the same thing, and music comes out of it.

Madame de St. Nicaise was adequate, but she wasn't that good, and she wasn't any good at all in making a graceful go of getting settled. She was dressed in the usual very full long skirt, which was of a fading bottle-green satin, and when Dr. Gollmer stood in front of her with the cello, while she got all arranged to receive it, it was a tableau straight out of Freud. If she had been a beautiful woman there might have been an exciting elegance about the whole thing, because Dr. Gollmer was being very courtly, but Madame de St. Nicaise was so plain and respectable, and her legs and knees, even through the green satin, were so obviously nothing more than acceptable utilitarian objects, that her action took on the quality of a public indelicacy as she prepared to embrace the instrument.

She really worked at playing that cello, though. The cello itself only tolerated her; they never did really get going together. But you certainly had to say for her that she gave it everything she had. As the concert went on she began to perspire freely. Stains appeared on the satin. She never let up

51

for a minute; she did everything she could to pull from the instrument everything it was capable of yielding; she seemed to surround it with a kind of heavy-handed loving encouragement. But she never did get any real music out of it.

She was under some very special difficulties that night, however. This was the concert which became famous in Léopoldville's social and musical history, the concert which began the Great Schism, which was the first severe blow in the series of blows which reduced Dr. Gollmer eventually to a desperate extremity, and which had to do with the death of Liliane Morelli. For a while, though, it seemed that this concert was doomed never to be performed at all. It was this preliminary crisis which resulted in my meeting Madame de St. Nicaise.

One morning a couple of days after Schmitty sold me the ticket, I was working in our office and one of the boys came and told me the Consulate wanted me on the phone. I went to it and said hello and Schmitty's voice said, "Good morning. An emergency has arisen."

I said, "Look, you're always bitching about me being overpaid and underworked. I'm working. No coffee this morning."

"It isn't that kind of emergency," Schmitty said. "Do you happen to have an E-string for a cello?"

"I might laugh if you said G-string," I said.

"I wouldn't."

"Neither would I. All right, what's funny about an E-string?"

Schmitty said, "The international situation's tenser'n all hell this morning. Madame de St. Nicaise has busted her E-string and she says it's up to your office to supply one, they being scarcer than hen's teeth in these parts, as the saying goes, and the duty of your office being one of procurement and supply. It's perfectly logical."

"Has she tried Brazzaville?"

"Every place."

"This is an office of strategic supply," I said. "I can't get the G-string gag out of my head. Now there's something strategic about a G-string—"

"I'm beginning to think you're overworked after all. Now listen closely: Madame de St. Nicaise has busted her E-string and if she doesn't get one by Wednesday night you and everybody else will get their fifty francs back and the whole goddam refugee relief program will fold."

"For a lousy couple of hundred bucks?"

"Listen, friend," Schmitty said, "we live in a ve-ry complicated civilization. Pull out one prop and you don't know *what's* going to tumble. Honest to God, Hoop, you've got to take her out of my hair. I can't do anything with her. You're bigger than I am."

"What am I doing, wrestling her?"

"I don't give a damn what you do. Charm your way out of it if you can. If you can't, civilization's got to crack, that's all. I'm through."

"O.K., what do I do?"

What I did, Schmitty said, was to go to her house.

"*Her* house!" I said. "Is she bed-ridden or something?"

"Or something," said Schmitty. "To wit, she has a grande-dame complex because of that *de* in front of her name. I know it sounds like a lot of you-know-what, Hoop, but honest, the old girl's on every committee and everything, and all that small-time stuff's just as important around here as it is anywhere else. More. Couldn't you possibly go out there this morning?"

"Well all right, but an *E*-string—"

"You couldn't possibly get one?" Schmitty asked. And if he could ask a silly thing like that, seriously, then I knew Madame de St. Nicaise wasn't just a small-time irritation. I couldn't even answer. Schmitty laughed at his end. "See how it is?" he said.

"Yeh," I said. "Well, I'll go out there. I don't know what I'll do once I get there, but I'll go."

"Thanks, Hoop. Give my regards to Madame de, won't you?"

"That I will, von Schmidt."

"And Hoop—"

"Yeh?"

"You're on your honor. Remember—she's a maiden."

"_____ _____," I said.

"*Dwacious!*" said Schmitty, and hung up.

The Morellis' front door was opened for me by a nice-looking houseboy in an impeccably clean white uniform of the standard type. He was barefoot, as the boys always are in respectable houses. The condition of their feet is an index to the efficiency of the ménage. This boy's feet were without deformities or amputations, a condition rarer than it sounds. They were as neatly groomed as a concert pianist's hands, with the nails nicely trimmed, the callouses rubbed down with pumice, and the skin softened and gleaming, like fine old furniture, from oil massage. He showed me into a living room and disappeared in a faint sibilance of starched cotton trousers.

I had time only to glance around me before Madame de St. Nicaise came in. It was a moderately large room of formidable gentility. The furniture was a mixture of awkward, expensive, 1920 Belgian pieces, completely without distinction, and some locally manufactured approximations of the same style. Each piece stood with merciless precision in exactly the spot from which you could tell it must not be shifted. There was a piano, a rarity in Léopoldville, and half a dozen pictures on the walls. One of these was a large, bad, academic-picturesque oil of a canal in Bruges; the others were dry, academic etchings of monuments in Louvain and Brussels, except for a single concession to Italian culture in the form of a tinted Alinari enlargement of a Lippi madonna, in the customary gilded-plaster imitation of a Renaissance frame.

Madame de St. Nicaise entered behind one of those smiles in which the lips retract charmingly from clenched teeth. These teeth had been cared for with the kind of dentistry which puts emphasis on utilitarianism rather than aesthetics, and it had taken a good bit of engineering to keep them in her head. Beyond that, she was not too bad-looking a woman at the routine level. She is hard to describe because her features were without individuality of any kind. She had a generous head of dark brown hair, beginning to streak into gray, parted in the middle and drawn back into a good-sized knot at the nape of the neck. The unexpected simplicity of this coiffure was the most attractive thing about her. There was a suggestion of heaviness to her face which went with her short, rather thick legs.

I had got as far as going up to the big oil to look at it more closely when she came in. I turned and she came up and gave me her hand, lifted only a little too high. I contemplated kissing it, and found the idea unpleasant so early in the day. My name is Tolliver, if I haven't mentioned it so far, and she said something like "Monsieur Taule le Verre" in the manner of a friendly grand duchess greeting a minor viscount and then, as I released her hand, she waved it elegantly to indicate the picture and said, "*C'est un canal de Bruges.*" If we were going to speak French, that would be an advantage; I could always hide behind my imperfections. She went on, still in French, "Ah, that Bruges! Down here, Monsieur, we suffer, isn't it so, we who have known the beauty of life."

As one lover of the beautiful life to another, I said, "But you have here a most agreeable house, Madame. It is a charming room."

"You find it so? Well, Monsieur, one does one's best under difficulties," but she was pleased.

We sat down on a sofa and talked for a while pretending that she hadn't got me there to get something out of me. I began to pick up a few cues. Since she was obviously fifteen years older than I was, a certain boyishness was required of me. If I could get down as low as ten, that would make her only twenty-five. I began to feel like an over-age juvenile in a bad amateur theatrical. But mostly she kept striking the note of exile, the duty (and privilege) of the cultured European (and, by sufferance, even the American who had risen above himself) to maintain the Spark for the other victims cast up by willful fate upon this savage shore. At the end of ten minutes, she was practically giving a symphony concert all by herself in a dugout canoe while I sat by and applauded.

When she really got down to business on the E-string deal, it became apparent that she really thought of this concert in terms of a major element in the Allied program. I don't mean that I don't thoroughly agree that it's admirable to have a string quartet in Léopoldville and I don't mean that I don't think it was admirable to make this concert a contribution to Belgian relief; I do mean that it was frightening, because insanity is frightening even in its most benign manifestations, to sit there and listen to this woman who in her own mind had contracted the dimensions of a global war to the scale of her own egomania. She saw no reason in the world why I shouldn't use the Consulate cable to locate an E-string, and get what in an offhand way she called "one of your airplanes" to fly the string to Léopoldville. And her attitude toward me as a person seemed to be that I was fortunate to have been called in to help in an emergency which not only gave me an opportunity to contribute to the war effort, but to meet Madame de St. Nicaise on terms of social equality as well.

As a matter of fact, there was the slimmest kind of chance that I *could* get the E-string. Our mail plane left that afternoon for Accra. I could ask the pilot to try for an E-string and send it down on the next plane that came our way, and although I'd feel like a fool asking a thing like that, it was possible that the errand might be accomplished. The returning mail plane wasn't due until after the concert date, but sometimes there were extra flights for one reason or another. It was the smallest chance in the world, dependent on other small chances all the way through, but I found myself giving in to Madame de St. Nicaise as I wouldn't have given in to a more reasonable person, and saying I would do my best, although I certainly did hate the idea of going up to one of those pilots and asking him to try to get me an E-string.

"Ah!" said Madame de St. Nicaise, "then it is all arranged!" She picked up a small bell from the table at her side and jangled it. The houseboy appeared immediately around the corner of the door with a tray bearing cups and saucers, a coffee pot, and some plates of little cakes. "Now we will celebrate," she said, and I wondered if I would have got my cup of coffee if I had said I was sorry but I couldn't do anything.

I had discovered that Madame de St. Nicaise had a passion for at least one creature—herself. Now I discovered another. There was a strange, harsh, resonant whining cry in the hallway, and a large Siamese tomcat entered the room. He paused to appraise me with a clear blue eye, but his flash of interest was momentary. He decided that I was both stupid and inedible, and crossed to the table, where he jumped suddenly with complete grace and precision, and bent his head to sniff at the cookies. He turned to Madame de St. Nicaise and yowled again, objecting in that odd voice, half rasping and half mellow, like a small accordion with laryngitis, that these damn cakes didn't please him at all.

"'Oh-la-la-la!" cried Madame de St. Nicaise. "Naughty Mimette! Pretty Mimette! No-no-no!"

Mimette regarded the spectacle of his mistress waggling her finger and talking baby talk, and swore softly under his breath. "Fool!" he muttered quite plainly, but when Madame de St. Nicaise patted her lap, he picked his way delicately across the table, not touching anything on it with so much as a hair of himself, and jumped down into Madame's lap and sat there facing me, with an air of complete indifference to both of us. I laughed, and he studied me again briefly, then yawned full in my face, displaying a fine ham-pink tongue with white bristles, and a set of needle-like teeth. "Laugh, you dumb bastard," he said. "It's three square a day."

Madame de St. Nicaise made cooing sounds and scratched him back of the ears and stroked him along the spine. She turned him over and subjected him to the indignity of a tickle in the groin. Mimette groaned in humiliation and turned his head away from me. Madame picked him up around the shoulders and raised his nose to the level of her own. He let his body hang like a sack of guts, but when she rubbed her nose against his he was unable to repress a slight tremor. "Kee-*ripes*," he said, and when she put him down on the floor he began stalking about the room, complaining rhythmically as he traced and retraced his path—up and over a chair, along the floor to the piano, up across the piano, threading his way through the objects on its top, down again, around the room, back to the chair, up and over, and so on, and at every fifth or sixth step he would give his particular hoarse yowl.

"Does he want out or something?" I asked. Mimette stopped dead in his tracks and gave me just one look, then went on pacing.

"Oh, yes," said Madame de St. Nicaise. "*Cher petit*, he always wants out." She said to Mimette, "*Doesn*'t he." "Jay-zuzz!" cried Mimette, and went out the door into the hall.

"Will the boy let him out?" I asked. He had looked so uncomfortable.

"Oh, no," said Madame. "We never let him out. It is very bad for cats here, you know," and when I thought of it, I realized that I hadn't seen any at all, except for a few mangy ones in the village. "Mimette is never out. He wouldn't know what to do."

Then she began on a complete biography of Mimette, all the cute things he had done as a kitten, all his childhood illnesses and how he had weathered them, the sweetness of his disposition and the aristocracy of his lineage, and so on. Mimette was a good guy and I liked him, but I wasn't interested in his life story. I was sick and tired of Madame de St. Nicaise and good and sore at myself for getting myself into the E-string business, and plenty ready to get out of there. I said, "I really must go, Madame. It has been such a pleasure to talk with you. I remember that I noticed you the other afternoon, with a charming young girl. At the Equatoriale."

Madame de St. Nicaise seemed to withdraw slightly, and her face maintained an ambiguous expression while she made a hasty effort to take her bearings. "Ah, yes, the Equatoriale," she murmured. Then, deciding where she was, she said with the faintest suggestion of playfulness, "I am afraid it was not the *best* introduction—not the one I would have chosen. Of course I seldom go to the Equatoriale—but there is no really good place. Everybody belongs to the Club now —everybody. One might as well go to a café. Of course, in Brussels—" and she left it dangling, suggesting a life of social elegance too rarefied for my experience.

"The young girl with you was very charming," I said, wondering whether it was within the bounds of human decency, even in association with Madame de St. Nicaise, to mention Liliane's grand entrance that afternoon. Madame looked at me again with the guarded, ambiguous expression; the conversation was taking new directions a little suddenly. Her eyes wandered from my face on down over my clothes. She seemed to be pricing them, and I half-expected her to reach out to feel the material of my coat-sleeve. Anyone could have read her mind, in a town where eligible young girls are a dime a dozen and eligible young men are hardly to be found at any price. Behind the ambiguous expression she began a concentrated scrutiny of details; perhaps this was not just another government clerk after all. I blurted suddenly: "What a charming day for me! Coffee with you this morning, and this afternoon I am having tea at the Governor-General's." It was true that we were going to the Governor-General's. It was a routine tea for the members of our mission.

Madame de St. Nicaise was too preoccupied with the luminous possibilities I had suddenly embodied to notice anything abrupt or inconsistent in my announcement. She took on the look of a cat who has just discovered that what he had thought was the same old beat-up cloth mouse in the corner was really a live and succulent one. She gave me that terrible smile again, but her teeth seemed to have grown larger, and all their metal re-enforcements took on a new conspicuousness.

"Yes," she said. "Yes—Jeanne, my niece." With deliberate effort she managed to relax. She rose and moved easily across the room to the piano; she had rallied. She said, "Come, let me show you her picture, pictures of my little family."

On the piano top were three photographs in frames which would have done credit to the Royal House if they had been replated at the corners. Madame de St. Nicaise stood before the tryptich and said, "Yes—Jeanne. She is a great comfort to me in my isolation here, Monsieur. She is pretty, don't you think?"

"Very pretty."

"And intelligent. A sweet child—and a pianist, too. Have you been much in Europe, Monsieur?"

"Yes, a little."

"Then perhaps you know our European girls. They are

not like your American girls, of course. Oh, your American girls are very pretty too—I am sure I would like American girls very much—although all we knew were the tourists, seeing them in the hotels and in the streets—but we of the old guard—to us it is always a little strange, the American freedom, which can have its dangers—for a young girl. Don't you think so?"

"Oh, yes. I think so."

"Yes," said Madame de St. Nicaise. She wasn't really getting enough help from me, but she kept on treading water. "Our girls, of course," she said, "have something—you do not mind my saying this, I know, Monsieur, you are so understanding of our beautiful things, so—I should not say this—so un-American in a way—do you mind?—I was saying that our girls, of course, come to marriage with something—something, after all, which your American girls do not have."

I said in English, "You mean a certificate of virginity?"

She said blankly, "*Pardon, Monsieur?*"

I said in French again, "I beg *your* pardon, Madame. I said, may I look forward to the pleasure of meeting your niece?"

"But of course that must be arranged," she said. "This is her father, Monsieur Morelli. You have not met him yet?"

The photograph of Morelli showed the face of a young man of about thirty, probably handsome, but so softened by hazy focus and the extensive retouching of the fashionable studio photograph of twenty years ago that it was hard to tell.

"Her father," she repeated.

Madame de St. Nicaise raised her hand and rested her finger tips on the top of the frame. The air suddenly seemed to grow still around us, relieved of the insistent commotion of her affectations. For a moment she was withdrawn from me, from everything except the photograph. I looked at her face; it had fallen into its natural lines for the first time since she had entered the room nearly an hour before. She looked straight into the eyes of the man in the picture; her lips parted slightly, and in the sudden quiet of the room the clattering echoes of her voice fell away, and I heard the sound of her breath, drawn in slowly, and released in a faint sigh. It was for only the space of that breath, but I had seen. She withdrew her finger tips abruptly.

I said, "No, I haven't had the pleasure of meeting Monsieur Morelli. I will look forward to it. He is in the offices of the *Appro*, is he not? Of course our office is concerned with them a great deal. He is a very handsome man. What you call your little family makes a very handsome group altogether."

"Yes," she said. "Of course, the photograph is quite old. It was taken in Brussels, before we came out here—as you can see. But he is still a very handsome man—and a man of very beautiful character, Monsieur, a man who takes the misfortunes of his—the misfortunes of life in a beautiful spirit. A beautiful spirit. This is Jeanne's mother. My dear sister."

I wanted very much to leave. The atmosphere of the room had become oppressive. For a while, with Mimette, Madame de St. Nicaise had seemed only silly. Now I felt an intensity and a troubling dislocation of proportion in everything she said, and I wanted to go.

"She is very beautiful," I said automatically, and, still without thinking, I said, "I shall look forward to meeting her also."

"But she is dead, of course," Madame de St. Nicaise said. "You know that she is dead."

"Oh, I am sorry. Forgive me. Yes, I remember now, it was the present Madame Morelli who the other afternoon—"

"At the Equatoriale," Madame de St. Nicaise interrupted me. "Yes." She had terminated the possibility of any further mention of Liliane. She walked away from the piano, back to the chairs we had been sitting in. "Will you have another cup of coffee, Monsieur? I must get it heated." She reached for the bell.

"No, thank you, I can't," I said. "I have kept you too long as it is. It has been so"—I thought I could say the word one more time without retching—"charming. I will do what I can about the matter of the string, Madame. I wish that I could guarantee a success."

"Thank you so much, Monsieur. We shall hope. After all, one can only do one's best." She seemed more reserved and reasonable than she had been all morning. She gave a little laugh and said, "Do you know Dr. Gollmer? No? He is the first violinist in our little quartet. A very odd man, but here violinists do not grow on trees, do they? No. Dr. Gollmer says he will make me an E-string. Can you imagine that? It is fantastic. Of course he knows how *ces indigènes*, these natives, make them for their own instruments, but I think he could never make one for my cello. Although he insists on trying. So we shall hope for your success."

"I will certainly do my best."

"You are very good," she repeated. She reached again for the bell, then she withdrew her hand and said, "No, let me show you out myself. You were good to come—very good."

I thought that if a moment's glance at the photograph of a lost love could make so much difference in a personality, Madame de St. Nicaise should look more frequently at the photograph of Morelli. As we approached the front door, Mimette came loping hopefully down the hall, and rubbed his side against my trouser leg. He yowled his odd half-harsh, half-mellow yowl, like an odd unseen bird—like a Siamese cat, impossible to describe, and he said to me, "Get me out of here, won't you?"

Madame de St. Nicaise picked him up. "No-no-no, Mimette." She smiled at me. "He always tries to leave with the guests," she said. "Naughty-naughty-*naughty* Mimette! Au revoir, Monsieur."

She lifted Mimette's face to her own, and pressed his jowl against her cheek. Mimette looked at me in degradation and despair, then in wild hope as I reached out to open the door. He struggled faintly, without any real conviction, in Madame de St. Nicaise's arms.

My hand touched the knob, but it seemed to come alive under my grasp, twisting of its own accord. The door opened from outside, and Mimette nearly slithered free. There was a moment of confusion as I stepped back to keep from being hit by the opening door and the young girl, Jeanne, paused on the sill. Behind her there was the silhouette of a big man, making an immediate impression of physical power through his sheer bulk. For an instant Jeanne's face took on an expression of surprise, but almost immediately she brought it under control. As many times as I saw Jeanne Morelli, and I saw her briefly and inconsequentially here and there many times during the following months, I was always brought up short by the unyielding reserve of her face, which was like a barricade for her to hide behind. It would be inaccurate to say that she was dead-pan, since the phrase has associations of stupidity, or to call her placid, which is certainly tied up with the idea of serenity. There was something a little sullen and something a little on the defensive at the same time in her expression, which seemed to recognize a pointlessness in her making any effort to interest you, and to deny the possibility of your interesting her by anything you did and said, although she was always polite and, in a purely formal and superficial way, attentive.

Madame de St. Nicaise introduced us as the door closed and Mimette's struggles subsided. Her niece, Jeanne; her brother-in-law, Hector Morelli; Monsieur Tolliver, the young man from the American Mission. She set Mimette down and he walked away listlessly down the hall. Now, said Madame de St. Nicaise, Monsieur Tolliver must certainly stay a few moments longer.

Jeanne and Morelli didn't seem to like the idea any more than I did, but we all moved back into the room, and as we went through a series of empty politenesses I tried to figure out where Jeanne Morelli missed fire. Her clothes were second-rate, but that was the rule in that locality during wartime, and they were in good enough taste. She had a beautiful figure, by the measurements, but something was wrong. She carried herself well—too well, maybe, because her body never suggested by any chance movement the possibility of its ever yielding. You could look at her and call her pretty or even very nearly beautiful, yet she remained so always in an oddly abstract and sexless way.

I kept feeling that if she would smile, just once, the whole person might warm up. Then I realized that she did smile, after a fashion, at the appropriate spots in what we were trying to pass off as a conversation, but the smile was as empty as the politenesses it recognized, and she remained hidden behind it, thinking whatever rather sullen and defensive thoughts it gave her satisfaction to cultivate. She was very young—only sixteen or seventeen—but her quality of unrelenting self-containment had nothing in it of the merely unawakened young virgin. She was awake, but she wasn't having any, thanks.

When I tried to describe this quality to Miss Finney, Miss Finney said to me, "Well, you know where it must come from, don't you?"

"I didn't then; I think I do now."

"Sure. You haven't any reason to think that she thought any different about Liliane's possible activities than other people thought, have you?"

"I guess not. Even the reverse. With Madame de St. Nicaise on the job, especially while the kid was growing up, she must have been subjected to some pretty good anti-Liliane propaganda."

"So Jeanne freezes to show the town that Liliane might be free and easy but that a real honest Morelli, of Morelli blood, wasn't only hard to get, but was impregnable. Not even interested."

"I suppose so," I said, "unless Madame dè St. Nicaise actually managed to induce a pathological frigidity. Don't you want to hear about Morelli?"

"Go ahead."

The impression of physical strength created by Morelli's silhouette in the doorway vanished when he came into the light and you saw him in the full round. He was a big man, and if you hunted for it you could still find indications of the fine Herculean proportions he must have had before his muscular flesh turned pasty, hanging as it did now, flaccid and in ruins, upon his bones. Of the handsome face in the picture on Madame de St. Nicaise's piano, only one feature remained intact: he had a nose with the kind of bony distinction which endures through any vicissitudes of bodily change, but the mouth and eyes were puffy and dragged out of shape in the general downward pull which culminated in his sagging belly. I am afraid this is a fairly unpleasant description to tag onto anybody, especially onto a man who didn't make that bad an impression when I met him. Morelli had a saving quality—a gentleness of manner which, however, was itself marred by a suggestion of discouragement and fatigue.

I was pretty sure I knew most of what there was to know about Madame de St. Nicaise, but I didn't have at all the same feeling about her niece and her brother-in-law. When you talked to Madame de St. Nicaise you got somewhere, even if it was somewhere you didn't like getting to, but with Jeanne and Morelli you didn't get anywhere at all.

Morelli, like Jeanne, was extremely polite, and he made

some exhausted efforts to sound hearty, since it was certain that in his job at *Appro* he would sooner or later have to do with me in my work at the American offices. My immediate interest in Morelli was a less creditable one. Here was the man who, by hearsay or truth, was the town's champion cuckold, and I felt a morbid curiosity about him. Whether his cuckoldry was a legend, as I suspected, or whether it was a fact, Morelli's air of faded vitality inevitably suggested it to anyone who had seen Liliane and felt her quality of urgent life.

But I can't really say that during the ten minutes or so I felt obliged to stay on at the Morellis' that day, I learned much about Jeanne or about Morelli, except what I could imagine about them from what I already knew of Liliane and Madame de St. Nicaise, and what you can imagine for yourself from the exteriors presented by people who are intent upon keeping themselves hidden from you. And I am willing to admit that perhaps I read more into two words I overheard Madame de St. Nicaise speak than was actually there. These words were simply, "Who knows?" spoken to Morelli. They said a lot, and in a way they answered their own question.

From where I sat, on the sofa near Jeanne, making words into sentences and exchanging them with her, but not doing what I would call talking, since talking implies some kind of communication—I could hear Morelli when he turned to Madame de St. Nicaise and asked, in a low voice, where Liliane was.

"Who knows?" said Madame de St. Nicaise, and although she spoke in accents of superficial patience and tolerance, I have never heard any words with more venom in them. I even wondered whether, with the kind of skill a woman like Madame de St. Nicaise can develop, she had not spoken with just the little bit of extra emphasis which would assure my hearing, and understanding, and elaborating for myself upon the disgraceful possibilities she managed to suggest in so simple a circumstance as Liliane's absence from home in the middle of a day which was no different from any other.

I told all this to Miss Finney, riding around after we had dropped Emily at the hotel.

Miss Finney said: "A couple of things, Hoop. You're usually a pretty clear reporter, but I don't get a couple of things. Where did the Morellis stand—socially, I mean. And where do they stand now, if they've changed. Outside La Belle Nicaise's delusions."

"Where they stood then and where they stand now is about the same thing," I said. "They're high-class second-raters."

"Oh, those," said Miss Finney. "I know the type. If they have aspirations they're the most uncomfortable people in the world."

"That's right. They never know for sure whether they're going to be asked to the best parties or not."

"Uh-huh. And they never know for sure whether they ought to accept their invitations to the lower second-rate parties or not."

"And they have a hell of a time with their own guest lists."

"Yes, like should they ask so-and-so and maybe get a rebuff, or should they just let it slide and maybe miss a chance to scratch their way up one more millimeter by their fingernails?"

"Should they drop so-and-so?"

"Add so-and-so?"

"If they get a good invitation, they don't know whether to mention it casually here and there, or lie low and hope word gets around that they were there."

"If they have a good guest list for a dinner, they don't know whether it's better to give it to the newspaper or go in for aristocratic reserve."

"They're all the time wondering just what quiet little parties go on that they don't even know about."

"Wait a minute," Miss Finney said. "Is this you talking, or me?"

"I don't know," I said. "I've lost track. Anyway, I guess you understand where the Morellis stand socially."

"What we're really talking about is Madame de St. Nicaise," said Miss Finney. "Do you think Liliane felt the same way?"

"She loved attention and needed companionship. I think she had a normal taste for social prestige. But mostly I think she loved friendly attention, no matter where it came from."

"What about Morelli?"

"Morelli was tired. I think he was so tired of being a battleground, with Madame de St. Nicaise charging over him day after day, that he was just lying down and taking what came."

"Jeanne?"

"Any young girl without anything to hope for but a good marriage suffers like hell from the party-list obsession. It's worse out here, with the ratio of girls to eligible prospects. You know that."

Miss Finney nodded in assent, but in the few seconds it had taken me to answer, her attention had wandered and now she tapped ruminatively against her chin with the nail of her forefinger. I didn't speak, but let her go on with whatever was occupying her, and shortly she stopped the tapping and said, "Hoop—of the various people closest to Liliane, how many saw her during the time she was sick?"

"Gollmer, of course," I said. "And Morelli. Madame de St. Nicaise. They nursed her. You couldn't get a nurse under any circumstances around here at that time."

"Why didn't they take her to the hospital? Crowded, I suppose."

"Full up. Then I suppose they didn't see any reason, at

first. I'm just guessing. But a routine case of malaria, even if it was a bad one. Then she was getting better pretty steadily."

"Who says so?" Miss Finney snapped.

"Don't you believe it? Why not?"

"I didn't say I didn't believe it," Miss Finney said. "I only asked who said so?"

"How do I know? That's what you heard around town, that's all. Everybody said it, I guess. Didn't you say yourself that it was on the records Gollmer showed you?"

"It was."

"Well, then."

"Forget it. Obviously the reports would have come from the old Madame, or Morelli, or Gollmer. But why didn't you mention Jeanne?"

"Because she wasn't here. She was here when Liliane got sick, but she wasn't here when she died. She didn't come back for the funeral, either, and it caused a lot of comment."

"On a lot of comment, phooey," Miss Finney interrupted.

"Yes, ma'am."

"Where was she?"

"South Africa. Is that important?"

"I've told you many a time that anything can be important. Why was she in South Africa?"

"They put her in school down there. Liliane took her down, and stayed there for a while. But Liliane had been back in town for some time before she got sick. Then Jeanne came home."

"Because Liliane was sick?"

"No, because there was some kind of vacation. She stayed over a few extra days because Liliane was so sick, but when she got better Jeanne left. Then immediately Liliane got this blackwater stuff and died three days later. I think it was three days. Do you want me to check for you?"

"Not now. Maybe later." She sighed heavily and said, "Give me a cigarette, Hoop"—a sign, from her, that the session was nearly wound up. "You know, Hoopie, it tires me out just to *think* of life in Morelli's house."

I passed her my cigarettes and matches. She took a cigarette, lit it, and handed the pack and the matches back to me. "Leave them on the seat," I said; there was somehow something comfortable in having them there.

Miss Finney took a couple of deep puffs and then settled against the back of the seat. "Sometimes, Hoop," she said, "when I've been working too hard, I ask myself why I've spent my life patching up a bunch of poor Godforsaken natives who don't know what the hell it's all about anyway. But when I think about lives like the Morellis', I think mine's been one long idyl. Lordamighty, can you imagine being Madame de St. Nicaise, and having Liliane brought into your house? All the hatred, frustration—"

"Always having to hide it."

"Every time she thinks she's clawed her way up that extra millimeter, having something like the Tiny business start going around town."

"Sitting at the same table," I said, "with Morelli and Liliane, and looking at Liliane and hating every yellow hair and every fine healthy pore of that body, and then going upstairs and looking in the mirror and seeing what she looks like herself, and going into Morelli's room and staring at the big double bed—"

"Wait a minute," Miss Finney said. "When did you see Morelli's big double bed?"

"I never did. I was just imagining."

"Well, you're getting a little florid," Miss Finney told me. "Don't overreach, Hoopie, you've got to stick to observed fact. Another thing I wanted to ask: was that an honest slip when you looked at that photograph and said you'd look forward to meeting Jeanne's mother, or were you just badgering the poor old she-dragon?"

"It was an honest slip. I'd only just come to town. I'd only seen Liliane that time with Schmitty at the Equatoriale, and maybe a time or two on the street or at the club. And the thing was, there wasn't a thing in that room, or a thing in anything that Madame de St. Nicaise said, that recognized Liliane's existence. As far as Madame de St. Nicaise was concerned, there wasn't any Liliane. I've thought of it often, since then—how Liliane must have moved around that house like somebody who had got there by mistake."

"I know, I got that," Miss Finney said. "You know, Hoop, when you were telling me this, I got about three different impressions of Madame de St. Nicaise."

"She acted like about three different people that morning."

"That's what I wanted to be sure of," Miss Finney said. "It's important. All right, go ahead now and tell me the rest of the E-string business. Then I've got to go home. Emily's always restless if I'm out late, and she needs the sleep. I'm listening."

CHAPTER SIX

I have said that Madame de St. Nicaise's uninspired performance on the night of the concert could be attributed to her being under some very special difficulties. One of these difficulties was a technical one, the other an emotional one. The emotional one was the death of Mimette. You may say what you wish about the performer who carries on in spite of a tragic circumstance ("Just before she went on, they told her in the wings that her husband had been run down by a taxi.") but it is not the rule that this inspires a great performance, especially if the part performed is not a tragic one, including, as this one did, anything as light in character as an arrangement of Chaminade's "Scarf Dance."

When I heard that Mimette had died, I felt bad about it, because in spite of his opinion of me and the dirty names he had called me I liked him, and also I thought it was a shame that as handsome a tom as Mimette had been should have died without experience of the world. I felt better when I learned the details, because Mimette had actually escaped out the front door at last, and his body was not found until five days later in the native village. The body was fairly fresh but in very poor condition, having been almost entirely devoured by scavenger birds. Most of the skin was there, however, and the head. Madame de St. Nicaise herself made the identification, but even if she had been unable to do so with certainty, it would have been safe to assume that the body was Mimette's, since he was certainly the only Siamese cat between Accra and Johannesburg. But I did feel better

73

about him, because he had been at liberty a few days living the fine, full, free life of uncloistered tomcathood, and if he had found any disappointment in what he had so long looked forward to, at least his curiosity was satisfied.

The trouble was that Mimette's death came at a terrible time for the Léopold String Quartet not only because of the fundamental emotional shock to Madame de St. Nicaise, but because she blamed the occurrence on Dr. Gollmer. There had been a rehearsal at the Morelli residence, and afterward when the guest members were leaving, Dr. Gollmer had carelessly opened the front door and Mimette, unnoticed among the confusion of feet and legs in the hallway until he had made good his escape, had slipped out. I never heard a firsthand eyewitness account of the scene that followed, and it is such an easy scene to embroider that the various versions I heard, some of which concluded with Madame de St. Nicaise laid out on the sofa in a rigor, aren't worth repeating, but apparently it was a scene of great unpleasantness.

The rehearsal itself had not gone well. Pending my delivery of the new E-string, Dr. Gollmer had shown up at the rehearsal with a raffia one he had made, which, being practically an *indigène* product, Madame de St. Nicaise could hardly bear to put onto her Caucasian cello, but she had finally used it as a desperate expedient. Its tone was very thin and not very true, so that she was at a terrible disadvantage, but at least a rehearsal of sorts had been gone through with. What with this irritation, and the culminating misfortune of Mimette's escape, Madame de St. Nicaise was in a bad state of nerves and depression. During the days of Mimette's absence she could not rehearse at all, and upon the discovery of his body, the day before the concert, it was decided to postpone the performance for a week because she was in no condition to play. In any case, she continued to insist that under no circumstances would she play on a raffia string, and an *indigène* one at that.

The postponement was an advantage to me in my assignment because it gave the mail plane time to arrive on its return trip.

It arrived, but without a string.

Although the *Voix d'Afrique* had not played the thing up the way, say, the *Daily News* might have if the story had hit during a dull spell, still they had begun carrying emergency bulletins on the concert, with really very nice tributes to the American Mission's efforts to locate a string, so nice in fact that I began to think I had missed a good chance at a public relations coup when I hadn't made more effort. By good luck, the pilot of the mail plane arrived with the news that he had actually tried to locate the string. I was able to give in all honesty to the editor of the *Voix* a story which he ran in a small box the next day, headlined: "*Tragédie Musicale: Pas de Cordes à Accra.*"

I thought that was the end of the concert, but on the following day the *Voix* carried a story with the headline, "*Le Concert Sauvé, Grâce aux Efforts de M. le Docteur Gollmer.*"

My first reaction to this headline was that it was a blunder, because Madame de St. Nicaise would be sorer than a boil if the concert came to be thought of as Dr. Gollmer's baby instead of hers, but the story took care of that very nicely, in a way that translates in a very rough way something like this:

CONCERT SAVED

THANKS TO THE EFFORTS OF DR. GOLLMER

The concert of the Léopold String Quartet, big event of the season, grand charitable gesture toward the unfortunates of the war, seemingly predestined to oblivion by a series of malchances—is rescued, thanks to the talents so generous and knowledge astonishing of the well-known local amateur anthropologist and writer extraordinary upon subjects native, Dr. Marcus Gollmer, and the most gracious agreeableness of our local lady musician most charming, Mme. Hélène de St. Nicaise. For, after many trials and errors painful, Dr. Gollmer has produced, with no more laboratorial equipment than the simple implements of his own kitchen, an E-string for the cello of Mme. de St. Nicaise, upon the formula for the strings of the lute Batshiok, which, while not the equivalent entire of a string proper, will serve two nights from now as the organ of transmission for the music so lively of Haydn, the melodies so charming of Schumann, the Scarf Dance so bright and so French of Madame Chaminade, and, grand climax, the beautiful dream so poetic of Debussy, composer impressionist.

Great thanks also to Mme. de St. Nicaise, patron of the arts and organizer of the quartet, who, through refinement of skillful musicianship and great courtesy of spirit, will accept the difficulties of performing upon this string extraordinary. To the civic spirit of this lady, our homages sincere.

Nor should we forget to render thanks to Monsieur Tolliver, of the Mission American, for the spirit of friendship in which he occupied himself with great efforts though unsuccessful, to procure by airplane a string regular.

To all we say, *Bravo! Well done!*

With this build-up the concert was a sell-out, and people came with an interest that couldn't have been much greater if it had been announced that Madame de St. Nicaise was going to manipulate the bow with her toes. The Haydn went off very well, and everybody was a little disappointed that the string didn't seem to make any difference at all. There was a round of what the *Voix* would have called applause lively, and the other musicians all bowed in the direction of Madame de St. Nicaise, smiling. Everybody was having a whale of a good time. But in the Schumann the string suddenly slipped so badly that the quartet had to stop, and Dr.

Gollmer came over and adjusted it for Madame de St. Nicaise, and they started over again, and got through without mishap, except for a couple of faintly sour tones that might or might not have been the E-string, I don't know. The first half of the program wound up with the Chaminade, which was arranged for four instruments by Madame de St. Nicaise herself, and a lousier bit of perfumed tripe nobody ever performed anywhere.

There was a surprise just before the intermission. It was announced that Dr. Gollmer would play a transcription of a Batshiok love song. He played this on only one string of his violin, a brief, wandering, gentle little line of melody that wavered through half and quarter tones and sounded thoroughly love-sick in the most appealing and touching kind of way. It produced far too much applause for the taste of Madame de St. Nicaise, who had sat on the stage back of Dr. Gollmer with an expression on her face that showed very clearly what she thought of native music.

A goodish number of people left at the intermission, and that was tough for them, because they missed the fireworks. The Debussy was too difficult a job for the Léopold String Quartet, and particularly taxing for the cello in the second movement, a slow sonorous melody with unexpected intervals in a curious, meandering pattern. Dr. Gollmer made a brief speech in the general tone of the *Voix* article, bearing down heavily on Madame de St. Nicaise's admirable combination of courage and musicianship which made her willing to tackle the job. She seemed somewhat mollified. The first movement went off all right, except that Madame de St. Nicaise sweated an awful lot.

They rested a moment before beginning Madame's ordeal of the second movement, and she and Dr. Gollmer fooled around with the string quite a bit. She seemed to be objecting to something or other; later, in her public statement, she said that she had noticed the wavering tone of the string and was reluctant to go on with the second movement. They began playing, though, and as the movement went on, the wavering tone was more and more apparent to everybody. The tone also seemed to be deteriorating in quality. She would draw her bow straight across the string, but the tone would change as she drew it, going a little up or down; also, the bow seemed to stick slightly to the string, as if the gut were not properly cured. It was some time during this movement that the horrid idea occurred to me that this *was* a gut string, not a raffia one, and that Madame's bow was being held back by a badly cured piece of animal intestine. The string wailed more and more irregularly. People laughed a little, but in a friendly and sympathetic way. But as the wailing grew worse, as it began to have a very particular quality half-harsh and half-resonant, as it began to suggest, in sudden uncontrollable yowls, the tone of a small accordion with laryngitis, my own spine prickled, and even from where I sat I could see the sweat drip from the forehead of Madame de St. Nicaise. She began to tremble; her eyes bulged. The other musicians regarded her in alarm, but she was unaware of them, even when they stopped playing. She panted, her eyes transfixed on her instrument. She drew her bow across it one last time; the string gave one final yowl, the very sound of an anguished Siamese. Madame de St. Nicaise dropped her bow and screamed, "*C'est Mimette! Mimette! My Mimette!*"

Then she staggered up, and the cello banged to the floor in front of her. She raised an arm straight out, rigid, and pointed a quivering finger at Dr. Gollmer.

"Murderer!" she screamed. "MURDERER! MURDERER! MURDERER!"

CHAPTER SEVEN

The repercussions of Mimette's death and possible trans-figuration into an E-string were at first public and highly colored. After the immediate hysterical ruckus had died down, the lives of Madame de St. Nicaise and Dr. Gollmer continued to be affected, in different ways, but both for the worse. The affair continued to exist as a kind of emotional cancer for Madame de St. Nicaise, and Dr. Gollmer's position in Léopoldville, through the efforts of Madame de St. Nicaise, was so greatly undermined that he was ultimately reduced to the position I have already described.

The simplest immediate result, and the most apparent one, was within the Léopold String Quartet itself. It was obvious now that Madame de St. Nicaise and Dr. Gollmer could never again enter the same room, much less appear on the same platform, to serve art or anything else. Dr. Gollmer was easily the best musician in the Quartet, but there were other amateurs in the city who had for years been yearning for admission into the group. Madame de St. Nicaise selected one of these for second violinist, promoting her second violinist to first to replace Dr. Gollmer, and then, incredible outrage, discovered that the second violinist of the original quartet preferred to stay with Dr. Gollmer, who was building a new quartet of his own. Eligibility for membership in either quartet came to be based on qualities other than musicianship, and since membership in Dr. Gollmer's group came to be less and less desirable as his position deteriorated, Léopoldville finally ended up with only one quartet, under

Madame de St. Nicaise, of course, where membership was determined entirely by the loyalty shown by its members to Madame de St. Nicaise during the schismatic period, and whose performances were at a level just as low as you would expect. But all this was relatively unimportant.

Open warfare between Madame de St. Nicaise and Dr. Gollmer began the day after the concert. Madame de St. Nicaise received her best friends at the Morelli residence, in a sort of day-long *levée*, propped up in a bed made with her best linen, and supplied with an endless chain of lace-edged handkerchiefs for eye-dabbers. The names she is reported to have called Dr. Gollmer during that day include brute, barbarian, cannibal (that one is a little obscure, but she used it), demon, ghoul, vivisectionist, and, in one bad slip into vulgarity, *espèce de chameau*. That evening, in response to the urgings of her friends (she said) she prepared a statement for the *Voix* (which had dropped the story like a hot potato), and when the editor asked her if she couldn't tone it down a little, she purchased advertising space in the paper in order to publish it as she had written it. Later it developed that the editor had shown the article to Dr. Gollmer and had received his permission to print it without action for libel.

For her statement Madame lifted from Zola: "*J'Accuse*," she called it. She accused Dr. Gollmer of having conceived the idea of using Mimette's gut as an E-string during the rehearsal when Madame had objected to the raffia string. She accused him of deliberately opening the door at a moment when Mimette was prepared to take advantage of the opportunity to scoot, of luring Mimette home with him, and there disemboweling him, with intimations that this disemboweling was done in some particularly fiendish manner (calling up images of an incision in the side of the living animal, from which the intestine was slowly drawn out to its full length), and of tossing the body in the street of the native village where what was left of it would be so despoiled by scavengers that its previous mutilation wouldn't be apparent. She called upon all Léopoldville—aye, upon the civilized world wherever men respected and loved animals, particularly animals of aristocratic lineage—to witness and to punish an act without parallel in the history of cruelty. She called upon the patron saints of animals to protect helpless beasts from worse beasts in the form of civilized man, and she ended by comparing herself, using every rhetorical device except the classical couplet, to the ancient king who was served the heads of his own sons on a banquet platter.

Dr. Gollmer's response appeared in a shorter, more direct statement the next day, also as a paid advertisement. He denied all knowledge of Mimette's whereabouts after Mimette had ducked out the door. He pointed out that Madame de St. Nicaise was apparently under the popular delusion that violin and cello strings are cat-gut, when as a matter of fact they are sheep-gut. He himself, however, had made the string in question out of the gut of a kid, on the formula of the Batshiok lute string, which anybody was at liberty to check for himself. He stated that he was willing to have the string subjected to any tests which would prove whether it was kid-gut or cat-gut, and to stand the expense of the tests himself. He offered the testimony of his houseboy, who had procured the kid-gut in the village.

At this point the *Voix* washed its hands of the whole thing, and refused to print Madame de St. Nicaise's rebuttal. But she circulated it by word of mouth. Of course Dr. Gollmer's houseboy would lie, would offer any testimony Dr. Gollmer wanted him to, she said. And of course you couldn't get anything out of any of the other villagers—*ces indigènes* were such brutes. If they weren't liars they would simply shut up and say nothing, even if they had seen Dr. Gollmer dropping Mimette's body in the street. As for the laboratory test on the string, you wouldn't expect her to keep the string around the place, would you? Of course not. She had burnt it, given it respectable cremation, the first thing the morning after the concert. No, she had *not* waited until Dr. Gollmer's offer of a test before burning it. She had burned it immediately: you didn't have to take her word for it, you could ask her house-boy, if you didn't believe her. It was too bad, it was simply too bad, that the murder of Mimette, which was as much a murder as anything could be, was not a murder in the eyes of the law and punishable by execution, that was all she could say. It was simply too bad. *But*, she would insist, at the end of her tirades, she wanted to make one thing clear, absolutely clear: as far as she was concerned, Dr. Gollmer was a murderer, and she would continue to regard him as one. That was that.

Dr. Gollmer was in a particularly vulnerable position in Madame de St. Nicaise's campaign to ruin his practice. I don't think he had ever been one of the best doctors in the world, by a long shot, and there had never been any illusions in Léopoldville on this score, but doctors were scarce there, particularly at that time, during the war, and Dr. Gollmer had an adequate practice. This practice was divided mainly between two groups in the city, the first being the very little people who would accept Dr. Gollmer as a doctor because his fees were smaller and because it was easier to get away with not paying him at all, if that was what you had in mind. The other group of patients called him in for exactly the same reasons. These were the low-class second-raters socially, a sub caste within the second-rate class of which Madame de St. Nicaise was a pinnacle. Among these people, who were as eager to have tea with Madame de St. Nicaise as Madame de St. Nicaise was to have tea at the Governor-General's, Madame de St. Nicaise waged her campaign. Ladies who had never entered the doors of the Morelli house except at large parties were received on terms of intimacy, and Dr. Gollmer began to discover that there would be whole days when he would not receive a call. Stories about him began to circulate around town. It had always been true that you couldn't depend on him, that he might go off to Popoka-baka without warning, and it was true that he often gave the impression of tossing off only a minimum routine treatment, on some kind of theory that most patients weren't worth more than routine attention, but now you also began to hear that he had prescribed a wrong dosage to so-and-so, and only the quick intervention of somebody-or-other who had *thought* a teaspoonful every hour seemed excessive, and had discovered it should have been a drop every hour—and so forth and so on. It made no difference if you listened to these stories with full knowledge that they were hearsay, and maliciously conceived in the first place. They affected your confidence in Dr. Gollmer and I, for one, wouldn't have called him in except as a last resort.

But what was happening to Madame de St. Nicaise was much worse. The emotional cancer was malignant. And long after people had tired of the story of Mimette, and had nearly forgotten it, and long after Dr. Gollmer and even Madame de St. Nicaise had ceased to analyze the source of the friction between them, this cancer continued to spread itself within her, and it occurred to nobody in Léopoldville, when Liliane Morelli died, that there was any connection between her death and the death of a Siamese cat some years before.

Miss Finney listened to the end of the story of the Great Stringed Instrument Schism without questions or comment, and when I finished she said nothing at all. We had wound in and out of town, and when I finished we were heading out into the country again. It had been a fine moonlight night, and now, at two in the morning, the moon was still brilliant. We rode on in silence for a while, until Miss Finney took a deep breath, shifted her position to sit up a little straighter, and said, "Thanks, Hoopie. Turn around now."

I stopped the car and finagled it on the narrow road to head in the opposite direction, and we started back to town.

Silence again.

I asked her, "Going to say anything?"

"I don't think so. Not tonight. You learn anything from telling me all this?"

"A lot."

"I thought so. How about breakfast tomorrow morning, Hoop? Come have it with Emily and me."

"Why don't you come out to our place, the two of you?"

"Fine. Fruit and coffee for me. Emily ought to choke down a little solid food, if you have it. What time?"

"Eight would be good."

"All right, eight." She paused a while, reflectively, and then eventually she said, "You know, Hoop, it's too bad that unpleasant people suffer so much. Makes you feel sorry for them when you shouldn't have to be subjected to any limitation of that kind."

"Maybe you're right," I said, "but I'd feel worse about having to feel sorry for Madame de St. Nicaise, unpleasant as she is, if I didn't feel sure that in addition to suffering quite a bit, she has also enjoyed some of the nastiest little satisfactions known to humankind."

"Many thanks," said Miss Finney. "That's the biggest word of comfort anybody's said to me for a long time."

I said, "Then we're out to get Madame de St. Nicaise?"

Miss Finney waited, the way you might do for a second or two before jumping across something you weren't quite sure you could make, and then said, "Yes. For the time being, yes. I could change my mind. One thing I'm pretty sure I want you to do, I want you to see Madame de St. Nicaise again, soon. Couldn't you pay a call of condolence or something?"

"That's something *I* don't want to talk about tonight. You know I'll do whatever you tell me to."

Miss Finney reached over and patted my knee. I usually got one knee-pat per case with Miss Finney, and this one having come so early, I knew things were going well from her point of view. That was all until we got to the hotel.

"Don't get out," she said, opening the door for herself. "Now you go home and get some sleep."

"I'll do that," I said, without any intention of doing it at all. "Give Emily my love. See you at breakfast."

Miss Finney climbed out and slammed the door. I watched her enter the hotel, then I started up and went in the direction of our quarters. But I didn't go there. I went a couple of blocks, just on the chance that Miss Finney might see me from a window, then when I was out of sight I turned off in the direction of the Funa, the swimming club, that is, because there was something special I wanted to think about. And the best way to think about it, considering that it was so special, seemed to me to be at two in the morning, all alone, in the bright moonlight, at the Funa.

PART TWO

CHAPTER EIGHT

If I had a favorite spot in Léopoldville, the Funa was it. It was a big pool, wide open to the sky, set out in the middle of great empty fields beyond the edge of town. As a pool there wasn't anything exceptional about it; it was just the usual concrete basin, with concrete pavement along the banks, and along one side this pavement was widened into a terrace to accommodate a scattering of tables under bright beach umbrellas. It wasn't at all fancy, but it was water to swim in. When you swam down into the bottom of it, it was cool. I used to swim around down there, rolling and paddling, as long as I could hold out. At one end of the pool there was a diving platform, with boards at ten, twenty, and thirty feet.

After I left Miss Finney at the hotel I drove through town and then along the rough deserted roads to the Funa's parking area, but the space looked so big and empty and quiet at night that the presence of the car there was like an intrusion. So I kept going, and took the little road or, more accurately, the pair of worn tracks that went off one end of the parking area, and bumped along past the bath houses and back of the other end of the pool. I parked the car in the shadow of the end of the bath house; that was better, because among other things it made my being there seem even more secret and made me feel more alone, which was the way I wanted to feel.

When I shut off the motor, and the last sounds of crunching under the tires had faded away, everything was absolutely quiet, without even so much as the sound of an insect anywhere. It was one of those silences which aren't just the absence of sound; the silence had an existence of its own, just as the air did, and both the silence and the air were impregnated with the vaporous moonlight, so that all three of them, silence, air, and moonlight, were the same thing at the same time.

I opened the door as quietly as I could, and got out, and shut it again without making any noise. There was the feeling that this silence and air and light shouldn't be disturbed, like the delicate pollen-like coating on the wings of a moth, that you wouldn't mar by rubbing your fingers across. When I walked toward the pool, the sound of my footsteps was absorbed quickly into the silence, and as I moved through the air it gave way before me and closed in behind me as usual, and the light, at once so brilliant and so unrevealing, lay quiet and undisturbed on my palm when I held it out and kept walking along.

I don't like to swim at night; it wasn't swimming I was after. I walked along the concrete terrace, past the beach umbrellas that were folded up and hanging in shapes like faded morning-glories, and followed the bank of the pool on around to the diving platform. This was a simple scaffolding of painted boards, and tonight it stood out as a criss-cross of bony white against the sky, with the diving boards projecting out blackly from it like stiff, flat tongues. I began climbing the ladder, prolonging the pleasure of ascent through all that light by going slowly rung after rung.

When I got to the top I walked out to the edge of the platform and looked out across the pool. It was black in the angle of the moon, but now and then the water would stir faintly, as if sighing in its sleep, and the surface would catch momentarily a slick heavy gleam. After a moment or two I turned away from the pool and went to the center of the platform and lay down on my back. It was completely isolated there. You couldn't see anything beyond the platform edge, and nobody could see you. It was more as if the platform were floating than supported from below.

I had spent a lot of time up there on top of that platform. Never at night before, but a lot of time, at high noon.

There's a story they tell in Africa and India and maybe other places; it's in most of the poorer tropical memoir and travel books, about the white man who went down at high noon to see his friends off on a boat, and forgot and took off his sun helmet long enough to wave them a good-by, and of course got sunstroke because he had let the noonday sun onto the top of his head. The noon sun was much feared and respected, and everything in Leopoldville closed up from noon until two, all the offices and stores and everything else, and everybody stayed inside, usually taking naps.

But if I take a midday nap, I'm logy for the rest of the day and awake for most of the night, so instead of fooling around our quarters I used to go all alone out to the Funa from noon until two. There was never another soul out there at those hours, never. It was fine.

I would jump in the water and swim across the pool and back, then go sit in the shade of one of the umbrellas and stick my legs out on a bench into the sun to try to get them brown. This was an experiment and a pastime, because I had never had brown legs and I didn't think it could be done. I know it sounds silly enough but this is the way it happened and I am telling about it. As soon as I got hot I would jump in and swim across and back and then sit there and sun my legs and heat up again. I used to do this for an hour or so every day.

My legs got brown as a Hindu's, and I even began to get an écru tone above my trunks, from the reflected light under the umbrella. So one day I said the hell with the story about the man who took off his sun helmet, and instead of sitting under the umbrella when I climbed out of the pool, I lay down on the bank, having to douse it with water first to cool it off, and I lay there until my hair was almost dry, on the theory that cool wet hair ought to do something in the way of keeping you from getting sunstroke.

I didn't get sunstroke, so from day to day I kept doing it more, jumping in and getting wet and then lying in the full sun until I was almost dry, over and over again. Pretty soon I began to develop the color of something in a beach advertisement, and like everybody else who has ever got himself a good tan, I began to look pretty silly to myself in the shower, with all the area under my trunks looking pasty and underprivileged.

This was in December, according to the calendar, at the end of my first year in Léopoldville, and that was the month I got my recall to come back to Washington. That winter I had a very special reason, which has nothing further to do with this story, for wanting to come home looking the best possible, and whether it sounds silly or not, for the sake of this special reason I wanted to capitalize on whatever associated ideas of romance and adventure were tied up with the word Congo; and the idea of coming back in the middle of December, to Washington, with a tan such as no one had ever seen before, was more than I could resist. And if you've ever really gone in for sun-tanning, you know that the sun-tanner's great yearning, the one thing desired above all, his dream of the sum of all good things, is to find a place where he can lie stark naked and get the same color all over.

So every day that month I went out to the Funa at high noon and jumped in and got wet and then climbed up to the top of the diving tower and took off my trunks and lay there in the sun. About every five or six minutes I would have to put on my trunks and climb down to the ten-foot level and dive in, then climb up to the top and do everything all over again, and before long I was the rich color of molasses, with a purplish sheen in the richest spots, all over. I really did a fine job, with oil and everything, and special attention to difficult nooks and crannies, and in the mornings when I would wake up, I would see the color I looked against the white sheet, and I knew that nobody, anywhere, without the help of walnut stain, had ever managed to transform his natural coloration to a greater degree or over a greater percentage of his surface area than I had done.

There had been a luxuriousness about those hours, lying up there, not able to see anything above, or around the four edges of the platform, except sky, lying motionless and feeling suspended in the blazing air. I had got to feeling that the top of that platform was my own, and one day when I went out and found another car already parked in the area, I had premonitions right away that there was a poacher around somewhere.

It was my last day. My bags were all packed and I hadn't a thing to do until I went to the airport after supper. I was feeling excited and a little sentimental, and above all I felt like lying there in the sun and not thinking, just feeling. This car wasn't a car I knew, and as I walked onto the terrace there was nobody in sight anywhere. But the water in the pool was agitated, instead of lying flat and smooth as it usually was when I first arrived. Then I saw that somebody had climbed out of the pool near the diving platform, leaving a wet trail that led right up to the ladder. As I started to climb, the rungs were still wet too.

I had seen from the terrace that there was nobody on the ten-foot platform, and when I got my head above the twenty-foot level there wasn't anybody there, and the rungs were still wet under my hands. I climbed on and stuck my head over the edge of my thirty-foot platform, and Liliane Morelli was sitting there in a dripping white suit, pushing her yellow hair back away from her face and straightening it a little by running her fingers through it.

She looked at me and smiled.

"Monsieur Tolliver," she said. We had met a number of

times. We had exchanged nods or even a few convention-
alities at parties. I had never danced with her, though, because I never did dance much, and when I dance I like somebody who is little enough to pick up and carry over the rough
spots. Also, I hadn't been sure I liked her.

"Madame Morelli," I said. "How did you get here?"

She kept smiling at my head stuck up over the edge of the
platform, and raised her eyebrows a little and made a gesture
with one hand to indicate the ladder. "I climbed," she said.
Her smile was beautiful—amused and very friendly, and her
teeth were white and beautifully shaped. "You forgot to go
in the water," she said.

So I had. I always drove out in my trunks and shirt. I had
left the shirt in the car but when I saw the other car there, the
rest of my routine had broken down. "How did you know I
always go in the water first?" I said. I had a sudden unpleasant feeling that all this time while I had felt so alone I had
been spied on.

"Oh, Monsieur!" she said. "Here, everybody knows
everything."

It gave me a start. Of course plenty of people knew I came
out there. Tommy Slattery and everybody else at the mission
knew it, and there wasn't any reason why they shouldn't tell
anybody they wanted to, but it was uncomfortable all the
same to find that people were interested enough to know it
and talk about it, even if it didn't mean a thing—or particularly because it didn't mean a thing. I had listened so
casually to so much gossip about Liliane Morelli that it was
uncomfortable to realize that all year people had been saying
whatever they wanted to about me too.

"What do they say?" I asked.

She laughed. "Nothing bad. That you come out here at
noon, that you jump in the water and then come up here and
sun *tout nu*, that you are as brown all over as you are where
we can see. That you will die of sunstroke one day."

"Not if I don't die today," I said. "I'm leaving tonight."

"I know," she said, in a pleasant, matter-of-fact voice. "Now you must get wet, or you really might get a *coup de soleil*." She moved her position a little to give me more room to climb up onto the platform.

It was an uncomfortable minute because I had never gone off the thirty-foot board and I intended never to go off it. I decided I wasn't going off it now. Male pride or no male pride I said, "Be back in a minute," and climbed down to the ten-foot platform and took my dive.

When I surfaced I looked up, and she was leaning over the edge of the platform. I realized that I was liking her. "Wait!" she called. She disappeared for a second, then reappeared and tossed a towel down toward me. "Bring it to me," she said. "*Very* wet!"

The towel hit the water and began to sink. I caught it, and heard her call, "And this. Fill it like a little bucket." Her white bathing cap came down. It hit the water with a faint slap and I got that too.

I swam to the bank and climbed out with the soaked towel dripping around my neck. I filled the cap, carrying it by its strap, and mounted the ladder to the top. She was smiling when I came up to the edge, exactly as before. When I had climbed over and sat down beside her she said, "Thank you," and took the towel and wrapped it around her head, turban fashion.

I have said I would hesitate to describe her as being really beautiful. But she looked really beautiful now. Even in the brilliant light there wasn't a flaw on her skin. It was gently tanned, but not tan enough to stand much of the sun the way it was at that time of the day. I was sorry about the turban. It looked all right but I had liked the look of her hair, wet and silky and curling a little, and glistening in the sun.

I said, "What do I do with this?" She took the capful of water and stood up, then moved over to the rail with it.

"This is for you," she said.

She hung it by its strap over one of the supports, then stood there looking out over the pool and the fields with the first houses of the city beyond them. But for me to see there was only platform and sky and Liliane Morelli standing in the brilliant sun.

I said, "What do you see?"

She said without turning towards me, "Nothing."

"Léopoldville?"

"A little of it."

"Don't look at it." With Madame de St. Nicaise, and Jeanne, and Morelli in it.

She turned her glance toward me, questioningly, and I said, "The nice thing about being up here is being away from everything else. When you stand up and look out, you lose it."

She turned full toward me now and said, "Yes. I know," and took the step or two to the center of the platform, and sat down close to me. There was a faint coolish scent of moist hair and flesh, very fresh and agreeable, mingling with the hot smell of the boards. Now everything beyond the platform was closed out again. She said, "Why, Monsieur? Don't you like Léopoldville?"

"I've liked it a lot. People have been awfully good to us." Although I was pretty sure I knew the answer, I said, "Do you?"

She looked genuinely puzzled, as if she couldn't decide. "It is hard to say. I have been so few places." She seemed to think about this, knitting her brows slightly. Then she decided. She smiled. "Of course I like it," she had decided. "I am quite happy here. Why not?" I smiled back at her, because I saw that even in her relationship with herself she was as naïve as she was in her relationships with other people. Our smiles held for a moment, then our eyes wandered in the inspection of one another by two people who have suddenly come on a new sense of one another's identity. Our eyes met again and she said, "You are really *épatant*, Monsieur. The color."

"I've worked at it. It gets to be an obsession. I want to get to Washington in midwinter this way. I'll be there in three days."

"How fine," she said. "I think you will make a sensation."

"I hope so."

There was nothing to say for a couple of minutes. When I would meet her eyes she would give me that smile, very frank and open and direct, friendly, but without any come-on. It was as simple and open as a good child's.

I asked, "Do you come here often?"

"Oh, yes. Very."

"Alone, I mean. I've never seen you here."

"I come at night."

"At *night?*"

"At night. If there is a moon. Sometimes when there isn't. When there is a moon, you can't imagine how beautiful it is. And more alone than ever."

"You like to be alone?"

"Yes, Monsieur." The smile went away and she added, "Not always, but sometimes it is very—" She stopped, and made herself stop thinking of whatever it was that disturbed her. She changed it to, "Sometimes it is very beautiful up here. When there is a moon."

I said, "My name's Hoop."

She considered this, and then said, "Very well. My name is Liliane." She added, "—Hoop."

I said, "Last day, first names."

"What?"

"My last day here, and we begin using first names."

She made no comment on this, but gazed at me rather questioningly for a moment or two before she smiled again and turned to pick up a bottle of some patented sun-tan lotion. She poured a little into the palm of one hand, set the bottle down, and began smearing the oily fluid onto her other arm. The oil darkened her skin to a golden color. I had seen that color somewhere.

I remembered. "Do you know what you're the color of?" I asked.

"No. What color?"

"The Parthenon. People think of it as white, but it's a kind of golden color. Pinkish in very early morning. Pinkish gold."

Her expression was a little guarded, and I wondered if she knew what I was talking about. "It sounds very nice," she said at last. "Pinkish gold."

"Except the Parthenon's a little spotty."

"Oh."

"Whereas you're not spotty at all."

She gave me that questioning look again. So far I had seen her use only two expressions, the smile and the question, but I liked them both. "Monsieur," she said, "I do not know exactly what this Parthenon is." Then the smile. "I called you *Monsieur* again," she said. "It is because I feel so ignorant. It is a building, isn't it? Oh, of course. There are many pictures of it. I remember now."

"That's right."

"In Rome. The big round one where the gladiators—" She sensed something wrong, and was quiet again.

"That's the Colosseum. You're not at all like that. Forget it."

"I am so ignorant," she said. "I make so many mistakes." She sighed and said, "Well—" but if she had anything else in mind to say, she decided it wasn't worth saying.

She was completely different from anything I would have expected. I wanted to ask her where she had grown up, how old she had been when she married Morelli, what she had done until then—or at least I wanted to know these things, but I didn't want to ask her because there was something too good about things just as they were. I was seeing her as I would never have seen her anywhere else—at the Equatoriale or at the Club—in a situation where she wasn't at the mercy of conventions and other attitudes she had never been taught correctly, and hadn't the subtlety to understand by herself. And since I was leaving, or because of the way I had felt when I came out there that day, or because of something, at any rate, we were talking as you seldom talk to anyone—without the fencing and subterfuge and self-presentation, or self-disguise, which are the basis of almost every contact you have with people, even if unconsciously part of it, because you are always trying, consciously or not, to fit them into the scheme you have for your life and the kind of person you want to present yourself as being, to the world. Sometimes on boats you're free from this compulsion; it accounts for boat romances, and the things that happen before the boat docks that could never happen after the passengers have got ashore. It's the isolation in place and also in time, because on a boat, what has gone before and what will come after are only half real. Up there, that day, it was like that, but reduced to some kind of final simplicity.

She said, "I meant to leave before you came. This morning I felt like coming up here."

"Don't go now. Stay."

"You are very agreeable," she said. "After all, it is your platform in a way."

"Mine at noon. Yours at night."

Then I said: "I like having you here."

She responded, "I like you." It came out perfectly naturally and for a second it was perfectly all right, then it became something that had got itself said unawares. For a minute we weren't quite alone. She turned and picked up the bottle of

99

lotion again, and was more careful than need be about pouring some of it into her palm. She began smoothing it onto her leg from the knee to the ankle.

I said, "That's good, because I like you too," but I had to say it as casually as I knew how, to make it all right. For another moment things hung in a balance; it could turn into a routine flirtation or it could go on being straight. What could she say, I wondered. If she said something silly or trivial, or on another tack entirely, it would be an acceptance of some embarrassment, and we hadn't felt any embarrassment yet; if she added to what we had already said, it would be making too much of it. We sat there as if we were listening to the sound of what we had last said. It began to sound all right.

She kept looking carefully at her leg as she smoothed it with her palm, up and down a few times, then she looked up at me with the smile, and instead of saying anything she offered me the bottle of oil. Then it was perfectly all right. We liked each other and had said so and that was that, and it was natural.

"No, thanks," I said. "I usually bring some, but I didn't bother today."

"But you will burn," she said. Then she looked at my shoulders and said, "No, I suppose not. But your hair is dry now."

She unwrapped the towel from her head and shook her hair loose, and felt of it. "I have more than you have," she said. "Mine's still wet." She left the towel off, and I was glad of it.

She reached out and touched my hair. "It *is* dry," she said. I felt it spring against her finger tips. I felt her parting my hair with her fingers, and for a moment she pressed close to the scalp. "It has dried through," she said.

"I don't want to go down," I said. What I didn't want to do was take any chance of disturbing things exactly as they were; I didn't want to admit there was anything beyond the platform, not even the cool water of the pool.

"You don't have to go down," she said. She rose easily, and fetched the cap of water, and came and sat beside me again. "This time I was careful not to look beyond the edge," she said. "It is so good here." She held the cap with both hands and offered it to me.

I said, "You do it."

She held the cap by its strap and with the other hand dipped a palmful of water on my hair. Then she laughed and said, "Too slow," and dumped the whole capful over my head.

I lay down on my back, arms and legs spread flat out. I had to crick my neck a little to look at her.

"You do need oil," she said.

"Give me a little."

She picked up the bottle to hand it to me, but halfway through the gesture she stopped. Lying on your back it's awkward to rub oil on yourself. She poured some into her palm and said, "Here," and began to smooth it across my chest. It was wonderfully luxurious. Then there was no question at all about what I was feeling. I closed my eyes and told myself that this was ridiculous and that I was about to make a mistake. At high noon, on top a diving platform, with a woman I had known about twenty minutes. But I knew it was one of the good times, not juggled and jockied for, unexpected, not even something important, but something more natural and immediate than you would ever find by hunting for it. I rolled over on my side toward her and put an arm across her waist.

"I like you," I said.

She didn't move, but remained there with the bottle of oil in one hand, and the other hand slightly raised, as she had withdrawn it when I turned toward her. We looked at each other, and I knew it wasn't ridiculous and that it wasn't a mistake.

She was the one who made the mistake. She wrenched herself away, not away from me because I made no effort to hold her. She wrenched away from herself, and stood up suddenly, where she could look beyond the edge of the platform and see the restricting world around her. She looked at me again, once, very quickly, and then disappeared.

I caught my breath as if I had been the one who had dived. There was a splash, then in a moment the sound of swimming. I heard the water stream off her onto the concrete as she climbed out, but I didn't move, lying there on my side, looking at the bottle of oil where she had dropped it.

"Monsieur?" from below.

"Yes?"

"I like you, too," she said, and before long I heard her car start and drive away.

But she had made a mistake. It would have been wonderful.

It would have been wonderful, and now, almost three years later, with Liliane dead, I lay up there in the night thinking about how she had been that day up there in the brilliant sun. I went over it all, just as it had happened, then lay there just letting whatever thoughts come that wanted to. I must have dozed, because I didn't hear any car drive into the parking area, and I hadn't noticed how low the moon was getting. I woke to soft voices and little splashings in the pool. I crawled over to the edge of the platform and lay flat on my stomach, watching the three figures playing around in the water—Gollmer and Mademoiselle Lala and Mademoiselle Baba, hardly visible except as amorphous silhouettes in the faded light, but unmistakably themselves. They were playing and splashing around in the shallow end of the pool; apparently the girls couldn't swim, for they only bobbed and bounced and splashed water at one another. Now and then one of them would jump as high as she could, splashing and laughing as she came down again. Dr. Gollmer would swim away from them, then come back, or climb out and dive back in and come up between them. I lay and watched as they played for twenty minutes or so; it was pleasant to watch, and I thought of the play of puppies. I liked it as an end to my long day, and especially as an end to the time I had spent up there thinking about Liliane Morelli. Watching them was like being part of the easiest and most affectionate companionship. Finally they climbed out of the pool and began wandering toward the parking area, where a car stood as a dark isolated blob. They spoke in low, gentle tones which I could hear without hearing the words, and finally I couldn't hear anything at all. I watched while they climbed into the car, and watched the car as it went out of the lot and down the road and out of sight. Then I got up and climbed down the ladder and went home. Mary Finney and Emily were due for breakfast in a few hours.

CHAPTER NINE

Three hours after I had got to bed, I turned off my alarm and rolled over and went to sleep again, and an hour later one of the boys woke me and said I had to hurry because they were almost through with breakfast in the dining room and there were two ladies this morning, *ung gran' rouge ay ung petee blanc*, he said, a big red one and a little white one. I staggered up and gave my face a few licks with the razor and staggered across the yard to the dining room.

Miss Finney and Miss Collins were sitting over coffee cups and Tommy Slattery was pinch-hitting for me and looking as if he enjoyed it. The breakfast table was a ruin, and everybody else had left.

I said, "Good morning."

"Where the hell have *you* been?" said Miss Finney.

I said, "Good morning, Emily."

"Good morning, Hoop dear."

"Good morning, Tommy," I said.

"Hiya," said Tommy in surprise. Our usual morning greeting was a surly exchange of grunts.

Miss Finney said, "You look like the wrath of God. What are you standing there for? Sit down and eat some breakfast. You're late."

"Good morning, Doctor," I said. I sat down and looked over the bleary half-papaya that nobody else had wanted and asked Tommy to ring for some toast. "In answer to your greeting, where the hell have I been, I have been the hell in bed."

"Well, you look as if you had shared it with a couple of chimpanzees," Miss Finney said. "I didn't keep you out *that* late."

"I fell in with some friends and we wound up at El Morocco."

Miss Finney snorted and turned to Tommy Slattery. "Mr. Slattery," she said, "I don't suppose you'd mind turning this wit over to me for the day, would you?"

Tommy grinned and said, "No, ma'am."

"You can go now, Tommy," I told him.

"As a matter of fact, I've got to," Tommy said. "It was a pleasure seeing you, Dr. Finney. Miss Collins. Why don't the two of you come out here to dinner tonight with us?"

"Thanks," said Miss Finney, "but I might be leaving town."

I said, "You might—*what?*"

"Be leaving town. Errand to do."

"*Good*ness," said Emily. "What in the *world*, Mary?"

"Little personal business," said Miss Finney, offhand. "Little business to settle up."

"But you will come, won't you, Miss Collins?" Tommy said.

"Oh, no," Miss Finney said. "Emily might be going too."

"*Good*ness," breathed Emily. "I might?" And then, philosophically, "Well—I'm afraid I can't accept your kind invitation, Mr. Slattery."

Tommy grinned again and said not to me, but to Miss Finney, "What about Hoop? Shall I expect him?"

"About that," Miss Finney said, "I don't know yet. Depends."

"I see," said Tommy. "Well, I'll be interested to learn what disposition you make of him. I'll have to excuse myself now."

"I'll keep you posted," Miss Finney said graciously.

"Thank you so much for the breakfasts, Mr. Slattery," and Tommy went out.

"This is dandy," I said. "I love travel."

Miss Finney made the sound which is usually written down as "Humph!" and went on, "Don't get your hopes up. For that matter, I might not be leaving, myself, or Emily either. Depends on how fast things go. There's so much to be done I don't even know what we'll do first. One thing, I want you to pay that call of condolence on Madame de St. Nicaise."

"Today?"

"This morning."

The boy brought toast and coffee and I almost choked on the first bite when I heard Emily say, "Poor dear Madame de St. Nicaise. I do hope the new Madame Morelli will be one she likes."

I heard Miss Finney take in her breath sharply. "Say again, please?" she said incredulously.

"Did I say something?" Emily asked.

Miss Finney said, "Emily, you are honestly the most—" She stopped, helpless. "Give me a minute to pull myself together," she said, and she literally did a little adjusting of straps or underpinnings or something of the kind as if her clothes had suddenly got out of normal relationship to her. Then she said, "You said something about how you did hope that the new Madame Morelli will be one that poor dear Madame de St. Nicaise likes."

"So what?" said Emily. She wasn't using it as a slang phrase. She meant she really wanted to know so what.

"Don't you think it's rather a spectacular announcement?" Miss Finney asked. "Two weeks after his second wife's death? Or did you just mean that you take it for granted that he'll take a third eventually?"

"Why, no," said Emily. "I mean this new one."

Miss Finney breathed heavily. "Where did you pick up

this bit of information?" she managed to ask. "And when?"

"Yesterday," said Emily. "At the meeting of the *Society for the Encourage—*"

"Et cetera," said Miss Finney. "Go on."

"—*Among Congo Natives.* Everyone there was talking about it."

"Everyone? Madame de St. Nicaise?"

"Oh, no, of *course* not Madame de St. Nicaise!"

"Hoop, have you heard anything about this?"

"No," I said. "For Pete's sake. It puts an entirely different light on the whole—"

Miss Finney shot me a glance that would have pinned me to the wall if I'd been against it, and I remembered that as far as Emily was concerned there had been nothing odd about Liliane Morelli's death. Miss Finney said quickly, "Emily, would you mind giving me this in more detail?"

"Now let—me—see," said Emily, like a conscientious little girl intent on giving the correct answer. "All the ladies of the committee were there, and Madame de St. Nicaise went out of the room for something. I was sitting over on the piano bench because I had just been playing 'Onward Christian Soldiers' for them and explaining how much trouble we always had with the boys at the missions because they keep changing the rhythm to their own, on the drums, and that had been kind of a mistake because Madame de St. Nicaise had said we shouldn't *allow* them to use their drums, not even with 'Onward Christian Soldiers,' and for a minute I thought I had lost us the pump-organ. She does hate native things so, poor thing. But then I explained to her that I *never* let them beat their own rhythms, but just a nice one-two-three-four, one-two-three-four—"

Miss Finney groaned.

"But you asked me how it happened, Mary," said Miss Collins, "and I'm trying to tell you. So she seemed somewhat mollified, and as you know, we *are* going to get the pump-organ, so everything came out all right after all. And then shortly after this, when Madame de St. Nicaise went out of the room, just the way I said, I was sitting there on the piano bench, and there were photographs on the piano."

"That's nice," said Miss Finney.

"I think so too," said Emily. "I love photographs on a piano. And one lady pointed to one of the photographs and whispered to the next one, 'This is the *first* Madame Morelli,' and another one whispered, '*No* photograph of Liliane, I notice,' and the first one said, '*What* is she going to say when she *hears?*'" Emily took a deep breath and started around the track for another lap. "And then the first one said, '*Poor Hélène,*' that's Madame de St. Nicaise, you know, and then another one came up and said, 'Poor Hélène why? What are you talking about?' and this first woman said, 'My dear, Morelli has had this girl down in Thysville for ever so long, and now he's marrying her. Everybody knows it,' and then" —Emily gasped like a swimmer coming up after setting an underwater record, and plunged again— "and then a couple of others came up and they all began whispering at once so I could hardly hear, and then Madame de St. Nicaise came in so they were all quiet again, and that's all. Is that what you wanted to know?" She sank back in her chair and I felt somebody ought to give her a rubdown.

"You did just fine," Miss Finney said. "Any better and I couldn't have stuck it out to the end. Emily, did this seem to come as news to the rest of the women, when they all came up and began whispering at once so you could hardly hear?"

"I think so. They seemed awfully excited," Emily said.

"I'll bet!" said Miss Finney. "Ghouls!" Her face took on a look of extreme concentration, which in her case means a look so dead-pan that you expect a membrane to slide over her eyes like a lizard's. Then she said, "Hoop, finish that toast and get out your best notepaper—have you got any good notepaper?"

"I've got the rest of the box that I had to buy to accept the Governor-General's tea party on."

"That's perfect. If only Madame de St. Nicaise could know that. All right, eat that toast, then get out that notepaper and write your prettiest note to Madame de St. Nicaise—for God's sake I wish that woman had a shorter name, I'm going to call her Nicky—about how Mr. Tolliver would appreciate the privilege of paying his respects this morning and send it over there by a boy in a spang-clean uniform right away. You sure you know absolutely the most proper high-toned form?"

"If I don't, I've been misled by the State Department."

"And send a boy with tattoo on his face if you've got one."

"Tattoo?"

"The G.G.'s messenger has the handsomest tattoo in town. We'll try to run second. Now go write that note. First tell the boy to put on his uniform and let me see him. The shape this mission lets its boys get into is a crying shame. Also you've got soap in your ear. Now hurry up. Do you realize it's going on nine o'clock?"

I did as she told me and came back after a while with the note for her to read. I was sure it was right because once I had had Schmitty give me the right form out of the Department social manual. I showed it to Miss Finney and after she had looked it over I said, "O.K.?"

"Hell, how do I know?" she said. "People don't write this kind of stuff to me. It sounds silly enough to be just fine. All right, let's have the boy. Where is he?"

I rang for the boy and he stepped in from behind the kitchen door where he had been standing stiff as a board in a new starched suit and he looked pretty good. Miss Finney sealed the note and looked at the address and then gabbled something to the boy in Lingala. He thrust his face forward toward her and bared his teeth like a leopard and half scared Emily and me to death. An uglier mouth full of choppers I never saw. "Fine," Miss Finney said. "Pretty good tattoo *and* filed teeth." She gabbled some more to the boy and gave him the note and he went out on a trot, beaming.

"What did you say to him?" I asked. "That's the first time he's smiled since he came here."

"I told him he had a fine set of teeth and I recognized his tribe from his tattoo," Miss Finney said.

"You're pretty bright," I said, meaning it.

"Oh, hell," Miss Finney said, "you pick that kind of thing up. You gave yourself a terrible shave this morning, Hoopie. I'll come with you while you do it over again. I want to ask you some questions. Emily, you go lie down somewhere."

"Oh, dear," Emily said. "Where?"

"Out of earshot somewhere. Hoopie?"

"There'll be beds made up in the guest room."

"That's good. All right—let's go."

We all trooped out, and went first to the spare room. Emily followed obediently, but just as we were about to leave her she said, "Mary?"

"Yes, Emily?"

Emily said with some asperity, "I do not intend to lie down. I am not tired. I have a mind of my own. I intend to sit up and read a magazine. Is that clear?"

Miss Finney's jaw dropped for an instant. Then she grinned and said, "Perfectly. See you later, Emmy."

As we went out, Miss Collins had picked up an old copy of *Esquire* and was settling down happily to puzzle it out.

CHAPTER TEN

We walked along toward my room, and as soon as I thought Emily couldn't hear us I said, "What about this stuff? This Morelli."

Miss Finney scowled and said, "I don't know what about it. It hasn't jelled."

"What do you mean, it hasn't jelled?"

"I mean I don't want to talk about it right now."

"What do you want to talk about?"

"I want you to get shaved and dressed and ready to go see Madame de St. Nicaise as soon as that boy gets back. Also I think now I'll go there with you. And Emily."

We went into my room and I went into the bathroom to shave. Instead of waiting outside, Miss Finney followed me into the bathroom and sat herself down on the rim of the tub. She sat scowling at first, as I began lathering up, then she seemed to dismiss from her mind whatever was bothering her, and became absorbed in watching me work with the brush.

The minute I had got my mouth covered with lather she asked, "Wonder what Freud or somebody says about shaving?" Just as I got enough lather wiped off to open my mouth she said, "Desire of the male to return to a state of innocence or something, I guess."

"The last thing I want back is my innocence. I had too much trouble losing it. The reason I shave is my beard itches in hot weather."

"The reason you shave is social pressure."

"Look," I said. "I'm trying to hurry like you said. Do

you want me to shave or talk? If you want to waste good shaving time by talking, that's all right with me, but unless the reason I shave really has something to do with what you're trying to find out about Liliane Morelli, we're not getting anywhere. Also you'll have to get off the edge of that tub or get splashed. I want a bath."

"Oh, all right. If you don't want me. I sort of like it in here, though. Intimate." She got up rather stiffly and straightened herself with the smallest bit of difficulty. "You're just trying to get rid of a fading missionary who has few enough sentimental pleasures as it is," she grumbled, "but I'll go. I'll be outside. And I do want you to talk. And if you change your mind and call me, I'll scrub your back."

She gave me a grin and went out. In a minute I heard the bedsprings creak, then a long sigh. "I'm listening," she said, and by the time I had finished shaving and bathing and dressing I had told her about the scandal of the "Congo Venus" as I had heard it first in letters from Schmitty, and in bits here and there after I had returned to Léopoldville:

Schmitty was a very spotty correspondent, and he spent a lot of what he did write in telling me how much satisfaction it gave him to know that I was sitting on my dead south-end under a palm tree doing nothing at all, with nobody to see me in uniform except a bunch of uniform-hardened Filipinos, since he always claimed I had been a chump and fallen for the glory-boy stuff when I went into the service. And he was perfectly right when he said that in one hour a day I could have done more for flag and country at my job in Léopoldville than I did during my total duty hours in the service, even if I had been able to fire an M-1, which Schmitty claimed to doubt. It was a great satisfaction to anyone who was 4-F on as many counts as Schmitty was, that nothing at all in the way of excitement happened to me while I was in the service.

Schmitty did admit that I was missed in Léopoldville, at least by him around eleven o'clock in the mornings, since he had been forced by the decimation of good company to take his daily *Kaffeeklatsches* solo, which certainly is no way to do a *klatsch*. He reported that the Equatoriale was "a vale of tears." And then he began writing me about Gollmer, who had always been somebody we knew by sight and reputation but, until then, not anybody either of us had ever had much to do with. He had coffee with Gollmer one morning and ended up by ordering a picture from him, although he said that Gollmer was drinking more heavily all the time to such an extent that a whisky-*klatsch* would have been more to the point.

Gollmer's picture-painting developed after I had left Léopoldville. When he became *de trop* among the local musicians, he turned to this Sunday-type painting for creative relaxation, and although Schmitty said that none of his pictures would ever make the Louvre, they had a certain interest, and Gollmer had a small local success with them.

In Léopoldville they used to hold a variety of charity auction that I haven't seen anywhere else. You would bid, say, ten francs on an object, and pay your ten francs into a pot. Then somebody would raise to, say, fifteen, and pay *that*, and so forth and so on, until finally nobody was willing to go above the last bid that was made (and paid) and the last bidder got the object, although nobody got his money back. These auctions were really brutal, and in his letters Schmitty complained that they had multiplied so that he was being bled white, it being his diplomatic duty to attend them, and the only thing that allayed his resentment was that he personally had almost got his money's worth out of them because he was lucky enough to be present at the auction of the "Congo Venus," which was the biggest scandal in town since the E-string fracas.

They asked Gollmer to donate some of his masks or

fetishes for the first of the series of war-relief auctions, but instead he donated a couple of his pictures, the first anybody had seen. The resemblance to Douanier Rousseau might or might not have been accidental, but Gauguin was definitely recognizable somewhere in the woodpile. Even so, the pictures were bright and direct enough to have some quality of their own, and the bidding was lively on them at the auction. The reason Schmitty bought his direct from Gollmer was that the old man was extremely hard up, with all his patients dropping away and most of what he did collect going for whisky.

It had come to be an accepted thing that a picture or two by Gollmer would be donated at every auction, and people began to look forward to their being put up. But when the particular picture called "The Congo Venus" was put up, there was a dead stunned silence.

The picture was a variation on Botticelli's "Birth of Venus," but the Venus was immediately recognizable as Liliane Morelli—standing, as Schmitty wrote, "stark raving naked" in the middle of the picture. Instead of Botticelli's shell she was standing on a big Watusi war shield floating up to the edge of the water, and instead of a nymph receiving her there was a long narrow Mont Hawa black girl wearing some blue beads, and she, Venus, was being blown along over the Congo by a kind of flying witch-doctor instead of the zephyrs or what not, with palm trees and pineapple plants instead of the laurel grove or whatever it is in the Botticelli.

It was a fairly big picture and was carried up to the platform in heavy paper wrappings. Then when it was unwrapped and people began to realize what they were looking at, the stunned silence was broken by a few small incredulous giggles, nervous, and then everybody began getting confidence from other people laughing until, Schmitty said, the whole room was roaring.

Then somebody yelled out *one thousand francs*, which was

around thirty-five dollars and unheard of for a starter, and actually dropped the thousand into the contribution box. Madame de St. Nicaise wasn't there, which was unusual; she was at home "with a headache" she said later, and Gollmer wasn't there either, but that wasn't unusual because he never came to the auctions anyway. But Liliane was there, not only there but passing the money box. Schmitty said she was fiery red, but the bids began coming in so fast that if she was trying to figure out what to do, she didn't have a chance, but kept going around carrying the money box from bidder to bidder as the bids climbed up around two thousand.

Then all of a sudden she froze and stared at the back of the room, and everybody in the place turned to see what she was staring at, and there was another sudden absolute silence as everybody sat craning around to look at Morelli standing up in the back row and leaning on the seat in front of him, ghost-white, trying to say something, and finally saying *ten thousand francs*, which was as much as he could be making in a month at his job.

There still wasn't a sound except a couple of little gasps and maybe, Schmitty says, a groan of pity from Schmitty himself, because he felt like giving one. He thought Liliane was going to buckle at the knees. Morelli began squeezing his way out to the aisle and she just stood there watching him, as if she didn't know whether he was going to knock her in the head or what, but she looked ready to take whatever he gave her. When he got up to her, he pulled out his pen and a scrap of paper and scribbled something on it—an IOU which he paid off later—and dropped it into the money box. Then he marched up to the platform and said *Wrap it*. Those were bad minutes, while they were wrapping the thing. Then he said *Bring it*, and turned his back on them and went back to Liliane. He said *Come, Liliane*, and she put her arm through his and they left the room.

The next time Schmitty wrote me he told me that Liliane

had been carted off to South Africa for what looked like an indefinite stay. Officially she went down there to put young Jeanne in school, but you heard everything, from divorce—which is a very serious thing indeed with the Belgians and would have made a real outcast of Liliane—to "amicable separation." All Schmitty could report, outside rumors, was that the daughter Jeanne wouldn't show her face in public and, presumably, had insisted on leaving Léopoldville for the school in South Africa; that Liliane tried once to brazen it out, one night at the Club, and got such an over-warm reception from the men and such a cold one from the women that you didn't see her around any more, either, from then on until she left town; and as for Madame de St. Nicaise, Schmitty said, she seemed to be everywhere all the time, hardly able to conceal her jubilation beneath a phony stiff upper lip.

Morelli looked haggard and distracted, and his work at the offices was so disorganized that everything he did had to be done over again by somebody else. This was at first. But a month or two later, after Jeanne and Liliane had been gone for some weeks, Schmitty mentioned that Morelli was looking a lot better, perhaps because he had been going on weekends to Thysville where, for whatever reason, he seemed to be finding some kind of relief from the pressures of his disturbed household.

CHAPTER ELEVEN

I want to take a minute here to point out something that might get lost sight of in going over this story. Telling it as I am, telling nothing about my life in Léopoldville except what had to do with the Morellis and Dr. Gollmer and the other people connected with them, it is easy to forget that my association with these people was very brief and casual and incidental. Even the business with Liliane Morelli on the diving platform was something isolated from the rest of my life at that time, and although I remembered it with pleasure and with some kind of affection for Liliane, it certainly was *not* one of the important things that happened to me, and it was only in going back and telling things to Miss Finney—or thinking them over to myself, as I did about Liliane at the Funa—that their importance seemed to increase, because I thought of them all together for the first time, in relationship to one another, as part of the same thing, instead of as unrelated fragments of my life in Léopoldville.

It has made some difference too in the picture of life in Léopoldville in general that I must have given here. The big comfortable houses, the parties at the consulates which really had some kind of elegance, the refugees who came with plenty of money and with a real experience of the things Madame de St. Nicaise only yearned toward and talked about—all these were a part of the city, but they were not a part of the story of Liliane, which I have been piecing together here as I did for Miss Finney.

In spite of what Schmitty liked to say about how little

work I had to do, we were busy at the mission, and on the nights before the planes left we usually worked all night without stopping. We went out a lot, too, and going to these parties was part of our job—not the Saturday night free-for-alls at the Club, but parties people gave for us, or official receptions and so on, and unless these were very big parties we never saw the Morellis or Dr. Gollmer there. And of course we were all of us involved in the kind of personal activities you are bound to get involved in when you live in a place a year and see a lot of people.

There were people in Léopoldville who became important to me, and there were people I got involved with much more seriously than I even began to be with Liliane Morelli, in spite of the feeling between us that day at the Funa. If that hadn't been my last day in Léopoldville, it might have been different. But as it was, Liliane and all the other people in the story as I had been telling it to Mary Finney—with the exception of Schmitty, because I saw quite a bit of him— were so removed from what I suppose could be called the main stream of my life in Léopoldville that during my time away from there I hardly thought of them at all. Eventually I would practically have forgotten all of them, if Miss Finney's curiosity about Liliane's death hadn't brought them all into focus with a new importance.

Take your own experience: right now you could think of somebody you know fairly well as an acquaintance, but who isn't important to you one way or another. But if there were suddenly a reason for you to gather together everything that had happened between you and that person, or that you had heard about that person, you might discover that it had a lot to do with this new thing of importance, and hence began to take on some importance itself.

The reason I am saying all this is that otherwise it might sound odd when I say that the visit Miss Finney and I had with Dr. Gollmer that day was really the first one I had ever had with him. We had met and that was about all. Also, considering what I had thought and felt about Liliane Morelli before I left, it would seem, in the light of this story only, that the first thing I would do when I got back to Léopoldville would be to look her up. But that didn't happen for the double reason that when I first got back, she was still in South Africa, and because by the time she got back herself, I was caught up in that main stream again and circumstances just didn't happen to bring Liliane Morelli into its current. She seemed much changed—much quieter, for one thing, although she didn't give me the impression of being chastened by the affair of Gollmer's "Congo Venus," and all the subsequent excitement, so much as she gave me the impression of having developed, for reasons I could only have guessed at, beyond the naïve social and emotional ignorance that had led her into such imbroglios in spite of what I was certain was a real innocence.

I tried to say this to Miss Finney, after I had finished telling her about the affair of the "Venus." If she had anything to say, she wasn't ready to say it yet. She looked impatiently at her big heavy wrist-watch from time to time, muttering about Madame de St. Nicaise.

I said, "What makes you so sure Madame de St. Nicaise will send back an O.K. for right away?"

Miss Finney said, "With Liliane dead only two weeks she won't be going out. She may be rejoicing, but officially she's mourning."

"She entertained the Society for the Et Cetera."

"That was different. She's President. And it's good works, not entertainment."

"Phooey."

"I know. You all ready now?"

"Sure. How do I look?"

She glanced at me indifferently and said, "Clean and healthy. Got a plain piece of paper and an envelope in here?"

"Plenty."

"I want some. Got another errand boy?"

"Paper, envelope, and errand boy," I said. "Another message?"

"To Gollmer," she said. I went to my desk and got some paper and an envelope and handed them to her, and she unclipped a pencil from her pocket and started writing. "No reflections on you as a reporter, Hoopsie," she said, "but I'm going straight to the source to get some more stuff about this picture thing. I'm sure I can manage Gollmer without getting him suspicious, and if he does get suspicious I'm sure I can convince him he should shut up. Call the boy, will you?"

"Do you want a clean starched uniform for this one too?" I asked.

"This one can go buck naked for all I care," Miss Finney said. I went to the door and called in the direction of the wash shed, and one of our boys named Alfonse came trotting up. When I turned back into the room, Miss Finney folded the piece of paper and handed it to me with the addressed envelope and said, "Read it before you seal it, if you want to."

It said:

Dear Dr. Gollmer—

I've been thinking over our talk of a couple of days ago and looking over the charts and so on you left with me. Have reached a decision and wonder if I can see you today. Since this is confidential and the walls at the ABC are thin, let's make it at the American Economic Mission, where I am just now with my friend H. Tolliver. Let's say 2 o'clock today unless you send a note by this boy saying no go, or unless you hear from me that something else has turned up, which isn't likely.

Yrs,

M. Finney, M.D.

"What might turn up?" I asked. I sealed the letter and gave it to the boy and told him what the address said.

"Chance old Madame might make a conflicting date, but I don't think so. Now I have something else to write while we're waiting, Hoop, and I want to sit at the desk and write it. Entertain yourself some way."

She went to the desk and sat at it, scribbling, scratching out, and so on, apparently really composing something this time. She was hard at it when the first boy came back with a note from Madame de St. Nicaise. She had received Monsieur Tolliver's charming note, hers said, and would be enchanted to be at home to him, and would receive him for morning coffee at eleven, or afternoon tea at five. She would expect a telephone call from him upon receipt of the note.

I showed it to Miss Finney.

"Eleven, of course," she said, "which means practically right now. Go telephone, Hoop. I'm almost through here. Tell her that charming Dr. Finney and enchanting Miss Collins would appreciate the darling opportunity and la-de-da-da-da of paying their respects at the same time. I'll be done with this when you get back."

I went over to the office and used the telephone, and when I got back, Miss Finney had collected Miss Collins, and they were both in my room waiting for me.

I said, "Hello, Emily, how'd you enjoy that copy of *Esquire*?"

"All right," she said. "After I figured out the first cartoon, the rest were easy. They all seem to be based on the same general idea. Mary says we're all going to call on Madame de St. Nicaise. Poor thing. I wonder if she's heard yet about Mr. Morelli and that girl in Thysville?"

"You'll know," I said, "the minute we step inside the door."

CHAPTER TWELVE

It was apparent from the minute we stepped inside the door not only that Madame de St. Nicaise had received no bad news of any kind recently, but that she thought she had her own mean little world by the tail. Her faintly house-keeperish air had vanished. She smelled strongly of perfume —a fresh, pleasant scent but inappropriate for her and too generously applied—and she was beaming all over the place, a kind of professional beam, it's true, but with some real beam back of it, not a beam of welcome so much as a beam of self-congratulation, and as she spread her lips at me I noticed that she had had some new dentures since that time I had talked to her about the E-string, and that they were a great improvement.

She had been doing some other things to her face, however, which were no improvement at all. If she had ever used lip-stick before, I had never noticed it, and she certainly was using it now. Lipstick is the biggest thing that ever happened for women, but somebody could have given Madame de St. Nicaise lessons in how to apply it and what color to use. She had a rather large, heavily muscled mouth, and she had made an awkward attempt to shape it and reduce its size, with a fuchsia-colored stick that brought out all the heavy sallow quality of her complexion. It was a color that would have been fine on Liliane, I thought—and then sickeningly I had a picture of Madame de St. Nicaise poking around in Liliane's things, smelling her perfumes—of course that was Liliane's scent—looking into jars of creams and lotions and sniffing at them, handling the brush and comb, unscrewing the lipsticks and sending their little fatty red ends in and out of their cases, and smearing them on her own lips.

And yet you go on moving and talking within the conventions, and I followed the three women into the living room, but I sat as far from Madame de St. Nicaise as I could, and to avoid seeing her I began examining the room, object by object. Except for the absence of Mimette stalking and yowling around in it the room hadn't changed a bit. I had certainly been right when I had thought that the position of every piece of furniture was rigidly determined. The chairs were still squatting sullenly in the same spots, and the photographs on the piano hadn't been moved an inch. Not one object had been added, and since Liliane's presence in the house had never been acknowledged by anything in that room, no object had been subtracted, either, but when I looked at Madame de St. Nicaise, and saw her purplish mouth moving in the opening pleasantries to Miss Finney and Miss Collins, it was as if the air were tainted with the odor of corruption. That's when you feel really thankful for the conventions, when you go on moving and talking within them, hiding behind them, and when I saw Madame de St. Nicaise's mouth moving at me, and saw it stop, waiting for me to move mine at her in the proper answer, I knew that I had been sitting there all the time with the proper expression, half smiling as if it were a pleasure to see Madame de St. Nicaise, and half solemn because of the occasion of the visit.

I said, "I was so sorry to hear of your loss, Madame. Permit me to extend my most respectful condolences."

Madame de St. Nicaise produced a lace-edged handkerchief from nowhere, like a magician, but she wasn't magician enough to produce a tear in her eye. She made a dry run, however, touching a corner of the handkerchief to the corner of one eye for a second, and then gently touching the bottom of her nose. She lowered the handkerchief and said, "Thank you, Monsieur. Thank you so much. You are very kind."

"I have not had the occasion to see Monsieur Morelli," I went on. "I hope that you will be kind enough to express to him my sincere sympathy in the loss of his wife."

"Ah, yes, Monsieur—yes. As soon as he returns."

"Is he away?" I said, surprised.

"Oh, yes," said Madame de St. Nicaise. "He is in Thysville."

"*Thys*ville!" I blurted. I looked at Miss Collins, who had said Morelli had a girl in Thysville, and I looked at Miss Finney, who had said she might be leaving town on a little business, but both of them sat there behind their faces and didn't show a thing.

"Why, yes," said Madame de St. Nicaise. "It is very restful there, and of course he has been under a great strain."

"Isn't that where the mental hospital is?" asked Miss Finney, who knew damn well where everything in the Congo was, and certainly every hospital. Madame de St. Nicaise looked somewhat taken aback, and Miss Finney said, "Oh, I didn't mean anything. I just mean it *is* restful."

I said, "It was very tragic for him. Such a sudden illness, and then—Madame Morelli had seemed so well. I had always thought of her as the epitome of good health. I found her a charming young woman, Madame."

Madame de St. Nicaise experienced a moment of facial paralysis labeled My Pleasant Expression for Use Under Unpleasant Circumstances. It was so painful to look at that I had to find something else to say, and I said, "How sad for Monsieur Morelli, to have lost two such charming wives."

It wasn't very good, but Madame de St. Nicaise relaxed her facial muscles and said with some animation, "Ah, yes, I am sorry that you did not have the opportunity to know my sister Jeanne, Monsieur, his first wife, of course. Such a charming gentlewoman, so quiet, so—what shall I say—so, ah, discreet, the very soul of gentility, Monsieur, with no thought but her home and her husband. Yes. It was my great good fortune to replace her"—she caught herself quickly and stuck in—"*partially*, upon her death. I came out here, Monsieur, to this wilderness, to care for the little Jeanne. Oh, I was mother to her, yes, and I did my best to maintain the home for Monsieur Morelli, although the sacrifice—"

She paused, and looked around at all three of us with what she used for a smile, and said, "But of course, for sacrifice one expects one's reward in heaven, is that not so? One does one's best," she said, and waved the handkerchief in an elegant gesture of dismissing the subject, then let her hand fall in her lap, "and looks for no other reward."

Miss Finney coughed and said innocently, "I see. And so now you have come back to Léopoldville to help out again."

"Oh, no," said Madame de St. Nicaise. "I stayed on after Monsieur Morelli's—remarriage."

"Oh, excuse me," said Miss Finney. "I'm a stranger here."

Madame de St. Nicaise said, "Liliane was so young and so inexperienced. Oh, yes, I stayed on, Madame, I stayed on and kept the house. The child Jeanne—I had become almost a mother to her, and it was for her of course the, ah, time in a young girl's life when she needs the, ah, guidance of—shall we say a wise, experienced hand? Oh, yes, I"—she made a gesture entitled Cheerful Renunciation—"stayed on."

"Goodness," said Miss Finney. "What a godsend for Mr. Morelli."

Madame de St. Nicaise smirked.

"And so of course you'll be staying on now, I guess," Miss Finney said, "now that the second Madame Morelli has passed on. We have a phrase in English. We say 'History repeats itself.'"

"Dear me," said little Emily, "you mean Mr. Morelli's going to get married *again?*"

Cripes! I thought, but I looked at her and she was playing it straight, all round-eyed. I looked at Miss Finney and she was sitting there looking sort of stupid and complacent, a manner she had assumed from the moment she entered Madame de St. Nicaise's door.

"Goodness, I wouldn't know," Miss Finney said. "Aren't we awful, sitting here in Madame de St. Nicaise's lovely living room and talking this way."

"Oh, but I understand perfectly," said Madame de St. Nicaise. "It is the frankness American."

But the thing was, that instead of jumping out of the seat of her chair when Emily had mentioned Morelli's marrying again, Madame de St. Nicaise had done nothing more than duck her head slightly, and then she began giving absolutely the best impersonation of the cat that had eaten the canary that I had ever seen. By God, I thought, she really does expect to be dealt in this time.

She went on, "Yes, you Americans are very frank, and it is charming, extremely charming. And as for Monsieur Morelli"—and she smoothed the material of her dress carefully over her thigh with the palm of one hand—"he is of course a gentleman, and always he can be depended upon to do what is for a gentleman *de rigeur*, but he is essentially a family man, yes, a family man." She sighed, and there was in it the quality of anticipation.

"My," said Miss Finney. "That's nice."

"And being a family man, of course," said Madame de St. Nicaise, encouraged by Miss Finney's response, "it is to be expected of him that he will continue the habit of domesticity. The home, the daughter—"

There was a hell of a blank moment in the room while nobody said "the wife," and then Miss Finney said, "Well, from what you tell me, Madame, he certainly is a lucky man to have *you* around."

Little Emily said in a voice like sugar and water, "A nice middle-aged man like Monsieur Morelli needs a nice dependable lady, maybe past her first youth. But you never can tell. So many men are so *funny* about what they pick out. Don't you think?"

I said, "Emily, for crying out loud!"

"Well, yes," said Miss Finney, "I guess there's such a thing as carrying the frankness American too far, but I certainly have enjoyed our congenial little chat, Madame. Well, I guess we'll have to be going." Everybody made a preliminary stir toward rising, except Miss Finney, and she caught me with my hind end half raised when she said, "Well, since Madame de St. Nicaise is so charming about Americans, I must admit I'd like to broach a subject, er, something special." She was being American as all hell, all awkward charm, and it stuck in my craw, but Madame de St. Nicaise said, maybe a little uncomfortably, "Of course, if there is anything I can do for you, Madame Finney—"

Miss Finney said abruptly, "Did you know I was a doctor? An M.D.?"

Madame de St. Nicaise jumped, I think we all did, and said, "No, I did not, Madame. I—ah—congratulate you."

"Thanks," said Miss Finney. "As a matter of fact, I've been gathering material on blackwater fever."

"Oh," said Madame de St. Nicaise. "Yes. I see."

"If you don't mind—" said Miss Finney.

Madame de St. Nicaise produced the handkerchief again, and holding it lightly to her mouth she coughed a couple of times, very phony.

"Pardon," she said graciously, "a slight phlegm."

"I'd like to give you something for it," said Miss Finney. So would I, I thought. Arsenic.

"How kind," said Madame de St. Nicaise. "But I have not much distress."

"I was saying," said Miss Finney, "that if it isn't too painful for you, if I could just learn some of the details, ask you a few questions—I know this must sound pretty heartless and so on, Madame, but you know scientists."

"Oh, yes."

"Well—maybe I'd better just forget it. I can get it from the doctor anyway. Who *was* your doctor, Madame?"

"*No!*" cried Madame de St. Nicaise. "To go to that man, Madame Finney—Docteur Finney—to go to that man, I would not wish that on *any*one. Now, Madame—Docteur— you are going to think it is *I* who am too frank. The frankness Belgian this time! This Dr. Gollmer—about Dr. Gollmer"—and now she was really breathing heavily—"about him I will tell you, gladly, yes, *very* gladly, Madame Finney. Oh, yes, I will tell you about Dr. Gollmer!"

"Well, yes—but I don't want to disturb you or anything."

"Disturb!" cried Madame de St. Nicaise. "You say disturb! But my dear Docteur Finney, you are not disturbing me! It is a pleasure, of that I can assure you! It is Gollmer who disturbs me! Disturbed! Yes, I am indeed disturbed, very disturbed, *but* about this Gollmer it is a pleasure to tell you, and I insist!"

"I see," said Miss Finney. "Well, in that case—" She turned to me and said in rapid English, "Hoop, you can sit back in your chair. It won't bite you." She turned back to Madame de St. Nicaise and spoke in French again: "Pardon, Madame. You were saying?"

Madame de St. Nicaise cleared her throat and settled herself in her chair, by which I don't mean that she settled back comfortably. She settled herself as she might settle herself in a saddle for an exhibition performance, and she began talking.

"For you, Docteur Finney, I will begin at the first," she said. "Now do not expect me to be tactful. Tactful I will not, I *will* not, be. In the first place I must tell you that long before this, I learned that Dr. Gollmer was a brute, yes, Madame, a veritable brute, who for the pleasure it afforded him—mark you, Madame, for the pleasure!—tortured animals. Oh, I could tell you a thing or two about *that*," she said, and as her glance fell on me and she began to recollect that after all I had known something about the Mimette controversy she looked for a moment uncertain, a little puzzled, as if even in her own ears the description of Dr. Gollmer as a man who tortured animals held the echo of an exaggeration which she had long since accepted as established fact.

But she glanced away from me, and went on to Miss Finney: "But about his past sins, and I assure you, Madame, that they are many, and of the most horrid—of his past sins let me not speak, but of this affair. Well, Madame, when Liliane became ill, I of course recognized the symptoms of the malaria. Oh, I had done everything I could, understand that, Madame, to protect the members of this little household. I have the records for anyone to see, of the daily quinine. But Liliane was very careless, you understand. She was young and if I may say so, she had never developed a proper sense of discipline in these matters. But I always saw that she had her quinine pill—yes, every day, and I have the chart, with each day checked, which I can show, for all my little family. But of course there are things which I can not always control. I can not be certain that Liliane always lowered her mosquito net at night. And sometimes she stayed out very late, of course, going to the dear Lord knows what kinds of places infested with mosquitoes. If she were ever near the native village at night, Madame, it is *ces indigènes*, ugh, the dirty things, who carry around this malaria, and of course a mosquito who bites one of them and then one of us— but I need not tell you, Madame, who are a doctor. But the idea—faugh! the blood from the native, and then to us—no, really, it is too much to think about!"

She paused for breath, and Miss Finney murmured, "Of course I see how you feel, but you could catch it just as bad from an infected white."

"It is too disgusting," said Madame de St. Nicaise. "But in any case I did what I could, of that I can at least take comfort, and when Liliane complained of the headache and fever, I recognized immediately of course what it was. We shall have the doctor immediately, I said, and my dear Madame Finney, I was too horror stricken when Liliane said to me that I must call Dr. Gollmer."

"What reason did she give for that?" Miss Finney asked.

"None!" said Madame de St. Nicaise. "But she was so stubborn! Ah, if you could have known my anxiety, but she insisted—no one but Gollmer. I said to her—to think of it now, to *think* that I said it to her, right then—'Liliane,' I said to her, 'but this is suicide! Suicide!' 'I will have him,' she said, 'and no one else.' So—what could I do? I called him."

Miss Finney sat there nodding her head like something mechanical and saying, "Mm-hmm, mm-hmm, mm-hmm," at regular intervals, so that she began to suggest some kind of small power device in operation to keep Madame de St. Nicaise going without loss of speed. Madame was really into her swing now, and she rattled away at a great rate, and the whole story had the sound of an exposition she had given over and over again to all listeners. But she still enjoyed giving it, and she told it with tremendous relish, although it was complete with gestures and grimaces which were supposed to indicate a wide range of emotions having to do with grief, resentment, pity, and righteous indignation.

"And so it was Gollmer," she said. "From the first I had presentiments of disaster. Because for a man like that to call himself a doctor is of course ridiculous—ri*dic*ulous! Now you know, Docteur Finney, for everybody knows, even we who like myself have cultivated the simplest knowledge of these tropical maladies, the simple home remedies and precautions —we all know," and here she accentuated each word by punching a thick rigid finger against her knee, "that *the— quinine—may—turn—the—malaria—to—blackwater—fever*. And so of course that is why I was always so careful that we should all have our pills daily, so that if the malaria came, we would be accustomed to the quinine in our systems. True? Am I not right? Of course. Oh, I can comfort myself that I did *my* part! And I said to Gollmer, 'Here, Monsieur'—for I never addressed him as Docteur, never—'here, Monsieur, here is the record of Liliane's quinine,' so that he could thus estimate the curative doses. And so! Even with my records, he gives her too much quinine, and—blackwater!''

She stirred eagerly, grinding herself firmly into position again on her buttocks, and leaning forward to look intently at each of us in turn. She resettled her glance at last on Miss Finney and went on in a low, ecstatic voice: "Murder. Yes. When it is a case like that—why should I be tactful?—I say murder. I say it for one and all to hear, yes, I will say it to Gollmer himself. I say murder. For as Monsieur Tolliver says, she was a girl who was the very embodiment of health itself. Never sick, never a day—strong. As strong and healthy,'' she said, and she took particular pleasure here, "as a peasant. Yes, like that. And when a man who has the temerity to call himself a doctor so treats the malaria that in a healthy peasant like Liliane the blackwater is produced— then I say it is murder, and that he is a murderer! Murderer, murderer—'' and her eyes were glittering.

I said, "But Madame de St. Nicaise, you can't—''

Miss Finney rose suddenly and said, "Well, we must go now, Madame. What I really need for my records of course is dosage amounts, a complete medical history, and so on. But I think we mustn't bother you any more right now.''

Miss Finney is usually pretty good at hiding anything she wants to hide, and she has no scruples at all about using this talent for purposes of deception, but I looked at her now and it was obvious that she was leaving because if she stayed any longer she was going to call Madame de St. Nicaise a goddam fool and a malicious gossip. Miss Finney is naturally a brightish red in the face, with a pleasant sprinkling of fairly large freckles of a darker shade, but the freckles were almost obscured now, the red of the rest of her face having grown as dark as the freckles during Madame de St. Nicaise's peroration.

Madame de St. Nicaise was a fool, but she wasn't so big a fool that she couldn't sense Miss Finney's anger. She said, "But Madame Docteur, I told you I could not be tactful."

"You certainly lived up to your advance billing," Miss Finney said bluntly.

"I have offended you, Madame."

Miss Finney seemed enough relieved by the one little jet of steam she had allowed to escape, so that she was able to say with adequate aplomb, "Let's not put it that way, Madame. Let's say that, uh, we have confused emotional issues somewhat with scientific ones. You were very good to let me come with Monsieur Tolliver this morning, and I can get the case records for my study from Dr. Gollmer. So I will say thank you and good-by."

We were all standing now, and it would be hard to say which one of us was sweating hardest. Madame de St. Nicaise said with real asperity, "Of course you are quite free to go to Gollmer, Docteur Finney. But let me assure you that I am a completely reasonable woman. The science—as you say, one understands the scientific attitude. And I have every record, every notation, on temperature, and quinine dosage— everything, from the beginning to the end. I assure you, Madame, you are quite welcome to them."

"Well, I won't ask you to get them now. They can wait."

"Very well. As you wish. You may rest certain in your mind that they are correct. Monsieur Morelli and I nursed Liliane ourselves, Madame. For twenty-four hours a day, between us. The records are the records we kept. It was certainly not easy. Monsieur Morelli was in a state of exhaustion, complete exhaustion, from the strain, and I—"

I looked in horror as her chin began to tremble.

"—and I," she said, "I have not had so easy a time of it!"

We stood speechless while Madame de St. Nicaise pulled out the handkerchief and really used it this time, blowing her nose violently. Then she caught her breath sharply a couple of times, and managed finally to say, "Pardon, Madame. I beg your pardon, all of you. Not for what I said about Gollmer. I will stick to that to the end. Brute! *Brute!*" She stopped again. Again she caught her breath, fighting for control, but she choked this time, and went over the edge. "Oh!" she cried, in a low half-howl, "Oh, I wish you had not come here! Go! Please go!"

She put her hand to her mouth and broke between Miss Finney and me, and somehow she made the door to the hallway and disappeared through it. We heard her go up the stairs, rapidly, with a heavy, irregular step. We heard a door thud closed. Then we just stood there.

"Damn!" said Miss Finney at last. "It never fails. They go and humanize themselves at the last minute and you feel like a dog."

Then she made a decisive movement, almost like an animal shaking itself, and the atmosphere seemed to clear a little.

"Come on, you two," she said, "let's get out of here."

When we got outside the house, it was like breathing again after you've had to hold your breath too long, getting past something that smells bad.

In the car on the way back to the hotel, because we were going there to drop Emily, we sat without speaking. We were all being extremely uncomfortable in our own ways, and the silence stretched out so long that everybody hesitated to say anything because after so much silence almost anything that was said was certain to sound inadequate.

It was Miss Finney who broke it, first with a *hmph* or a kind of grunt which was half amused and half disturbed, then she said, "Well, Emily, there goes your pump-organ."

"Oh, I gave that up a long time ago," Emily said, "as soon

133

as I began to see you and Hoopie were up to something."

"Indeed?" said Miss Finney.

"In*deed*," said Emily. "And you're just taking me back to the hotel to drop me and get rid of me so you can go around meddling some more. You must think I'm awful dumb, Mary," she said plaintively, "just because I *used* to be."

"I know what you're after," Miss Finney said, "but you're not going to get it. You want to get in on this because you hope you'll get another chance to shoot my forty-five. Well, nobody's going to get shot this time so you might as well get that notion out of your head." She looked at Emily with half a grin and said, "I never thought to see the day I'd be warning Emily Collins against the use of violence."

"Violence or no violence," said Emily, "I know very well what you're up to. I'm not going to ask you any questions, I wouldn't want to give you that much satis*fac*tion, but what I want to know is, have you got any kind of official standing?"

"That's a very attractive deal on the questions," Miss Finney said. "The answer is, no I haven't. None whatever."

"Well!" said Emily.

"Unofficially, but for general information in case by some chance some small wispy friend and fellow missionary worker of mine should let some cat out of some bag—unofficially, I've done what I've done because a friend of Dr. Gollmer's came to me and asked me to make a statement that in my opinion Gollmer had done all a doctor could do, and that it wasn't his fault Liliane died—that she'd had the treatment any doctor would have given her, and she'd have died under anybody else's care just the same. For Gollmer it's a matter of professional life and death. And I haven't said or done a thing so far that couldn't be explained on those grounds, if I found myself with any explaining to do."

"Well, I think Dr. Gollmer's horrid," said Emily. "Two

girls at once, and all that whisky. Are you going to give him that statement?"

"As a matter of fact, I think maybe I am, in one form or another. By the way, that was another question."

"Oh, *Mary*," said Emily. "I'm not a *baby*! And I won't be pushed off, either. If I'm going to"—and she shot me a glance, wavered for a moment, then went on—"going to do what you asked me to last night, I *will* ask questions. I'll ask one right now: you've talked to Madame de St. Nicaise. Do you really think she killed Liliane?"

"Yes and no," said Miss Finney.

Emily said, "I think you're mean."

"I'm not mean," Miss Finney said. "You wanted to know what I thought, and I told you."

"But it's the most obvious thing in the world," I said. "I've got it all figured out. She didn't give Liliane quinine tablets, she gave her something else, like those bicarbonate-of-soda tablets that look just the same, the ones like Tommy Slattery's that I took for so long, thinking I was taking quinine. She didn't give her the quinine, just hoping she would come down with malaria."

"Oh, is that the way it was?" Miss Finney said.

"It could be," I said.

"Why of course!" Emily chimed in. "*I* saw that much, and I'm not even clever."

I said, "And then when Liliane actually did get malaria, the dosage Dr. Gollmer prescribed was too big, because he went by those records Madame de St. Nicaise had faked and he prescribed for a system accustomed to quinine. Liliane probably hadn't had any for a hell of a while—certainly not since she got back from South Africa and maybe she didn't take any while she was down there, either. So it gave her blackwater."

"Of *course*," said Emily.

"Let me point out right now," said Miss Finney, "that there's a major fallacy in what you're saying, both of you."

"What is it?"

"I won't answer that question. If you'd done everything I suggested, Hoop, you'd be seeing a little clearer."

"But what didn't I do?"

"I won't answer that question either."

"What didn't I do?" Emily asked.

"For one thing, you haven't followed my medical career very closely," Miss Finney said, "but that's all right, I haven't followed your articles in the *Missionary Survey* very closely either."

I said, "But if Madame de St. Nicaise didn't do anything to Liliane, are we all through? That 'yes and no' stuff. Do you give Dr. Gollmer his statement, and we're all wound up and finished?"

"Certainly not."

"Morelli?" I asked. "Gollmer?"

Miss Finney's answer to that was a shrug. Then, "If you're listing possibilities, you might list the possibility that I'm also including, and including very seriously. Liliane Morelli might have died a natural death."

I had a feeling I didn't want to recognize, even for myself, but I sat there and felt it for a minute, then there was no possibility of refusing to recognize it, and I admitted it. I said, "Maybe it makes me a mean-spirited louse, but I'm just plain disappointed. I'd got so accustomed to thinking of Madame de St. Nicaise as a murderess that I don't want to deprive her of the only interest she had as a person."

"You've got a very delicate point there," Miss Finney said.

"What's delicate about it? She's duller than dishwater unless she's bad."

"I mean about whether she's a murderess or not."

"Look," I said, "will you make up your mind?"

"Here's the point, Hoop," Miss Finney said. "She wanted

Liliane dead; she tried to kill Liliane; she thinks at this minute that she succeeded in killing Liliane. If that doesn't make her a murderess I don't know what does. But I'm not sure she killed Liliane, no matter what she thinks. Suppose Emily wants to kill somebody. Make it, uh, Madame de St. Nicaise because she's snatched back the pump-organ. Emily goes and takes a shot at the old girl. But for reasons too complicated to figure out for this analogy, let's say the old girl wasn't even hit by Emily's bullet, died of something else. Legally I guess Emily isn't a murderess. But morally she is and morally is what really counts, the law being only an effort to standardize in applicable form a group moral code. Where are we?"

"Up where the air's too thin. All I want is for you to answer yes or no or shut up to a few review questions. One: at this moment you don't think Madame de St. Nicaise killed Liliane?"

"Maybe so, maybe not."

"But she herself thinks she did?"

"Yes. Maybe she knows it for certain."

"And you're unwilling to elaborate."

"Unwilling."

"Ultimately, what are we aiming for?"

"Ultimately, a confession from Liliane's murderer, if any. And that, my dear Hoop, is my last word for now."

"That's all?"

"That's all."

"In that case, we're forgetting about lunch. Let's eat."

"We've got forty minutes for it," Miss Finney said. "Dr. Gollmer at two o'clock."

CHAPTER THIRTEEN

Miss Finney and Emily and I had lunch together at the ABC after we left Madame de St. Nicaise, a hurried lunch, no dessert, and at eight minutes to two Miss Finney pushed her plate away and said, "Hoopie, we've got to shove off. Emily, there's work you can do."

"Oh, dear," said Emily. "I'm scared."

"Nonsense," said Miss Finney. "You'll do just fine. You did just fine on Hoopie—"

I said, "Huh?"

"—and you'll continue to do just fine elsewhere. You remember your itinerary."

"But Mary, if anything *hap*pens—"

"Emmy, I tell you again, *don't worry so!* If anything goes wrong I'll get you out of town fast. Are you tired? Do you want to lie down a while first?"

"No, if I've got to do it, I might as well begin now." She went through the equivalent of girding up her loins, which meant plucking nervously at the hem of her skirt, rose, said "Well—good-by, then. Good-by, Hoopie dear," sighed, looked uncertainly down the street, said "Well—" and tottered off.

I said to Miss Finney, "Of course it's none of my business what it was that Emily did just fine on Hoopie."

"Of course not," Miss Finney said. "Hurry, we'll be late for Gollmer."

She scribbled her name and room number on the check, said "Nonsense" when I protested, and we started to the car.

I said, "Also I suppose it isn't any of my business what kind of villainy you've set poor Emily about this afternoon."

"None of your business at the moment, but something you practically suggested to me yourself."

"*When*, for—"

"Yesterday. Don't bother me, Hoopie."

As we drove out toward my place I said, "How are you going about this talk with Gollmer?"

She said, "I don't quite know. I'm just deciding, or trying to. If you'd be quiet and let me figure it out. I'll get started somehow and manage it whatever way seems best. Now just let me think about it a little."

"Well, all right. But I sure am beginning to feel pushed around."

She reached over and patted my knee, which made twice in two days, a record.

"You're getting soft in your old age," I told her.

"That's what you think. You'd be surprised."

"I'm in a perpetual state of amazement," I said. "All right, go ahead and think. I'll shut up."

"You know Mr. Tolliver, Dr. Gollmer."

"Yes, we have met several times. It is very agreeable to see you again, Monsieur."

"Pleasure, Doctor."

"Hoopie'll be here for our little talk. You don't mind? You can tell him anything you'd tell me."

Dr. Gollmer hesitated, making this adjustment, then said, "Of course. Whatever you say, Dr. Finney."

"Without beating around the bush, Doctor," Miss Finney said, "I might as well tell you I'm going to ask you some questions out of just plain female curiosity. I'm just plain curiouser'n hell about a couple of things and I can't stand it any longer."

Dr. Gollmer gave a big smile and said, "Extreme curiosity

is a form of pain. The function of our profession being in part the relief of pain, I will be glad to do for you what I can." When he smiled, his harried old face took on some of the vigor it had had when I first used to see him around town.

I said, "Shall I have some drinks brought in? What would you like, Dr. Gollmer?"

He hesitated again, and if he didn't lick his lips, he gave that impression. Miss Finney said, "Oh, go ahead, Doctor. Let's relax. I might even have a little one myself. Let's have some whisky, Hoop. O.K.?"

I went to the door and called for a boy, and gave him the order. When I came back and sat down, Miss Finney had an envelope in her hand, and was giving it to Dr. Gollmer. "I don't know whether it'll be exactly what you need," she was saying. "There's no point in pretending that you treated the case just as I might have treated it myself. I said exactly what I could say in good conscience, and no more. I said that you gave the customary treatment which the patient would have received under most doctors but I made it pretty strong that my statement was made dependent on the accuracy and completeness of the records given for my inspection. I had to do that, Doctor. I made it as emphatic as I could without saying something I suspect—which is, that there were complications in this case that the records don't indicate."

Dr. Gollmer was silent. He looked extremely unhappy, and his mouth went a little more out of line than it ordinarily was. He began, "The complications in this case—" and he wanted very much to go on and say something further, but he stopped himself with considerable effort.

He changed course and said, with a directness that made you like him, "Perhaps I am not the best of doctors, Dr. Finney. But this case seemed so extremely simple. I say, seemed. And it is true that I gave it the simplest, the most routine treatment. You are extremely good to give me your statement, especially since it was extremely presumptuous of this mysterious friend to ask you for it. If you are giving it to me with any reluctance at all, I hope you will feel free to change your mind and take it back, without feeling any embarrassment."

"Don't worry," Miss Finney said. "I'd never put anything in writing I wouldn't expect to stand by the rest of my life. And as I've said, I've protected myself with reservations and so on." Her voice had been very matter of fact. Now there was the slightest change in it, a relaxation, just the smallest suggestion of an invitation to confidential exchange. "I can see how the case seemed extremely simple. I can only guess at what the complications might have been," she said.

Whatever Dr. Gollmer had wanted to say before was almost more than he could keep from saying now. There was a distraction while Alfonse appeared with a tray of glasses and whisky, seltzer, plain water, and ice. Dr. Gollmer's eyes followed not Alfonse but the whisky bottle on the tray, from the moment Alfonse entered the door until he set the tray down on the table beside me.

I said, "Miss Finney?"

"Very small," she said. "Plain water, lots of ice. Just flavor it." She smiled at Gollmer and patted her abdomen and said, "Have to go easy. Upsets me these days," which was a black lie.

"Dr. Gollmer?"

"A little whisky over some ice, please," he said. It was already a generous drink when he said, "No, no—enough!" and I let some more spill in after that.

The minute I had poured myself a drink Dr. Gollmer raised his and said, "Your health, Dr. Finney. Mr. Tolliver."

"Yours," Miss Finney said, and took a sip from her glass. Dr. Gollmer took a couple of hefty swallows from his, and for the first time since he had sat down he leaned back in his chair. I had always liked his looks, with their combination of a kind of mauled elegance and casual disreputability, and as the whisky began to relax him, these qualities became more pronounced. It was easy to imagine him, as it hadn't been when he first came in, playing and sporting around at the Funa, in the waning moonlight, with Lala and Baba, as I had seen him doing only a few hours before.

The conversation was general and meaningless for a while. I don't think ten minutes had gone by before Dr. Gollmer passed me his glass and I filled it for him again. I made it another heavy one. I handed it to him and he began chuckling.

"Well, Dr. Finney," he said, "*and* Mr. Tolliver, this is very pleasant, very pleasant indeed. There is something Dr. Finney wants to know, and old Gollmer is being reduced to a state of complaisance by Mr. Tolliver's hospitality." He looked at me and I felt myself reddening, but Miss Finney just grinned and said, "I told you I wasn't going to beat around the bush. I don't know whether I can explain to you exactly why I'm interested in what I'm going to ask you, or not. Just put it down to female curiosity, won't you? It's about Madame Morelli, Liliane Morelli. Not as a medical history—as a person. The more I hear about her, the more she interests me."

Dr. Gollmer sobered somewhat and said, "*La pauvre petite*. What do you want to know about her?"

"Well, first let me tell you I was talking to Madame de St. Nicaise this morning."

Dr. Gollmer took a particularly long drink. He lowered his glass and said, "You could not have heard anything very pleasant."

"What I heard was very *un*pleasant," Miss Finney said. "I'm afraid the session ended with something like hard feelings. But she told me one thing. I hope you don't mind my asking, and I hope you won't be offended when I tell you that it seems extraordinary to me that Liliane insisted on having you as her doctor. Madame de St. Nicaise was very agitated. Apparently she tried to argue Liliane out of it, and Liliane was adamant."

Dr. Gollmer held his glass out in front of him and seemed to study it carefully. Without looking at either of us he said, "I am not sure, Dr. Finney, but that I might be a little offended by that question. Or rather, I feel that I *should* be. Can you give me any good reason why Liliane, or anybody else, shouldn't call me in as their doctor?"

"Certainly I can," Miss Finney said, "and so can you. Madame de St. Nicaise has waged a persistent whispering campaign against you—"

"Hardly in whispers," Gollmer corrected her.

"Well, you understand the methods she's used, at any rate. That's one good reason why some people wouldn't call you in, and it has nothing in the world to do with your ability as a physician. And the reason Liliane wouldn't be expected to call you in hasn't anything to do with your ability either. You know very well what it has to do with."

Gollmer handed me his glass. It was empty except for ice. "Fill it for me again, young man," he said. "Fill that glass for old Gollmer. And when I ask you to fill it once more, fill it, and after that, no matter whether I ask you or not, don't give me another."

I put in another couple of chunks of ice, and poured whisky over them to fill the glass. It was a good four-ounce drink at the very least. Dr. Gollmer accepted it with a nod of thanks, held it up to the light, squinted at it, and murmured, "Beautiful. Beautiful."

Then he took a preliminary sip, and set the glass down on the table. He reached into the inside pocket of his coat and withdrew the letter Miss Finney had given him. He handed it to Miss Finney and said, "For you."

"But Dr. Gollmer—gosh, I hope I haven't made you feel—"

"Not at all. Take it, Dr. Finney. You should never have been asked for it, you should not have felt obliged to write it, and I should not have accepted it. Please take it."

"But—"

He held up his hand, still offering the letter with the other. "Take it," he said. Miss Finney took it, with what I am certain was genuine reluctance, and looked at Dr. Gollmer questioningly.

The old man picked up his drink from the table and settled back in his chair. He closed his eyes for a moment, then opened them and smiled. "I feel much better," he said. "And now I can talk freely. Oh, I know that the letter was not any kind of payment, advance payment, for information you would like to have; and I could have accepted it without feeling that I had to give payment, in case I had felt able to accept it at all. But now without question I can speak freely, more freely. You say that I know perfectly well why it seems odd that Liliane should call me in. Of course I do. You are thinking of the affair of the picture of Liliane, the 'Venus.' But what I also know is why it was not odd at all—given her sweetness of character—that she should insist on having me. Are you certain that none of this will embarrass Mr. Tolliver?"

"I'm certain it won't embarrass him and I'm certain he won't repeat anything you don't want him to repeat."

"Very well. Now for your sake, Dr. Finney, let me describe to you a scene in Léopoldville, on a certain night, when one of the Ladies' Group auctions is being held. I was not there, for the very good double reason that it is a stupid way to pass an evening, and that I have no money to waste on bids for useless objects. But I have heard the evening described many times, with malicious relish by my enemies, or sympathetically by my friends, and I have made it a point to create for myself the clearest picture of that auction. Now you must imagine the hall crowded with the best people in town, and with people in town who are not the best, but who like to be in the same room with the best, even if they must buy their way in at an auction. You must imagine Liliane passing the money box for the bidders—Liliane because she is pretty, she is obliging, and the sight of her puts the men in a good humor when they must pay their bids. The objects begin to come up, one after another . . ."

Dr. Gollmer went on to describe the scene at the auction. He nursed his drink along, going slowly on it since he had only one more to look forward to. He told the whole story of the sale of the picture to Morelli for ten thousand francs, and told of Morelli leaving with Liliane. At the end he passed me his empty glass without comment, and I filled it without saying anything either and handed it back to him, and put the cap on the bottle.

He went on: "Now you will ask, why was old Gollmer such a fool as to paint such a picture in the first place? Well, my friends, it was a poor picture, a pretentious failure, a mistake. But you see I had begun painting these little pictures. In a way I had had a certain success. They always went well at the auctions, and some people in the city bought others from me, and seemed to enjoy owning them. There is a great pleasure in creation, and greater pleasure in gaining recognition, no matter how small. Now old Gollmer is not quite a fool, but—have you ever painted? My little success was so unexpected, and the pleasure of painting was so great, that I became ambitious. I wanted to do something—oh, I was very mistaken—something beyond the simple landscapes and genre scenes of native life which had occupied me. I conceived this very bad picture. I had always admired Liliane, as a beautiful object. She was a great joy to look at. She was beautiful, Dr. Finney. You never saw her, but she was very beautiful—not in your drawing-room fashion or

your movie-star fashion. She was not one of your manne-
quins. She was a beautiful woman because she was so natural,
a great simple magnificent girl in full blossom, and with a
skin—! She was beautiful. And so for my bad picture, my
'Congo Venus,' I thought of her. Like every man in Léopoldville, I—well, let us drop that.

"I do not like even to deny that Liliane posed for that picture. Of course there was never a question of that. I would
never have asked her and she would never have thought of
such a thing. But when gossip spreads as it has spread, it
becomes necessary to deny that Liliane posed, although even
the denial, even this negative recognition of slander, is
offensive. She did not pose.

"For the head, yes. And that was a mistake on my part,
to ask it, but not on hers to comply, since she did not know
that it was to be more than a head. But it was a mistake on
both our parts that she came to my house. It was like Liliane,
obliging and innocent and thoughtless, to come. Obviously
I could not enter the Morellis' house; it was Madame de St.
Nicaise, not Liliane, who said who should and should not
come there, and after the affair of the cat—" He made a
gesture of amusement and resignation.

"So she came to my house. I made a sketch, on paper, of
the head, in perhaps an hour. She did not see the painting at
any time, she knew nothing about the painting. I never intended that anyone should know about that picture. It was
an exercise, a secret pleasure for old Gollmer, who imagined
himself becoming an artist and doing a salon picture, working on the sly like a little boy practicing a stunt in secret,
where his friends cannot see his awkwardness and his fail-
ures. In the painting I put Liliane's head on the goddess, and
I fabricated the figure from my postcards of Botticelli and
Rubens. That is the story of the 'Congo Venus,' which in
the course of events I would have destroyed before long,
because it was a poor picture. Although old Gollmer had

been fool enough to conceive it, he had the sense to look at it when it was finished and know it was bad."

The whisky, and his interest in his own story, had at first brought a life and animation to Dr. Gollmer's face, but now he looked tired again, and his face looked not so much relaxed as fallen in, and he not so much leaned back in his chair as sagged back in it. His glass was empty, and he looked ruefully at the capped bottle. I thought of Ulysses tied to the mast, and thought that the worst thing that could happen to me at that particular point would be for him to ask me to give him another drink after all.

I think he would have, too, if Miss Finney hadn't stopped him by saying suddenly, "Dr. Gollmer—I'm interrupting with a question—but how did Madame de St. Nicaise get hold of that picture?"

Dr. Gollmer tore his eyes away from the bottle and turned to her and said, "You know that?"

"I deduce that. I know that she didn't attend the auction, and I know that she's one of your not-quite-the-best, and that even if she had a roaring headache or anything else, if she'd had two broken legs she'd have dragged herself to that auction to cash in socially on her share of it—if she didn't have more to gain by staying away. And all I can figure she had to gain was the certainty that the picture would come up for auction. She knew it was there, but if she attended the auction, say if the picture were unwrapped beforehand and she saw it in the presence of other people— she'd have had to see that it didn't get put up, and *that* she didn't want to take a chance on having to do."

Dr. Gollmer said, "Dr. Finney, in my position I have to try to say as little against Madame de St. Nicaise as my self-control will let me."

"Don't you think you can carry the business of behaving more or less like a gentleman too far?"

"Of course, but—"

"In this case, you allowed Madame de St. Nicaise not only to harm you by getting that picture up, but you let her harm Liliane too."

Dr. Gollmer said, "Don't correct me, Dr. Finney!" but he said it not angrily, but pleadingly. "I was in an impossible position! The original mistake was mine, in painting the picture at all, and the harm was done by the time I knew about it, so I took my share of it, instead of adding to the gossip by bringing in Madame de St. Nicaise too. I might have helped myself—although I don't think so, Dr. Finney; people who want to gossip will always believe an evil rumor instead of a creditable one—"

"That's what Mr. Tolliver says. He says drop a couple of rumors and give them an equal start and see which one comes out ahead."

"Exactly," said Dr. Gollmer. "It wouldn't really have helped for me to insist exactly why I feel certain that the picture was put up for auction through the manipulations of Madame de St. Nicaise, and it would only have added to Liliane's misfortune. It would still have been a picture of her, and the fact that Madame de St. Nicaise was carrying on a nasty family intrigue would only have made Liliane the center of a further nastiness."

"But you did deny, publicly, that Liliane posed for it."

"Over and over again. I denied that Liliane knew anything about it."

"Which was true."

"Of course it was true!"

Miss Finney said, "I seem to be asking questions instead of just letting you talk."

"Please," said Dr. Gollmer. "Please do. I am tired. It is easier that way."

"Then what story does Madame de St. Nicaise tell as to how the picture got put up for sale?"

"Oh, she tells a good story!" Dr. Gollmer said, "and a

148

story I have no way of refuting. You see the Ladies' Committee had asked me for some pictures, as usual, and I had agreed to donate some. After all it is a good cause even if the means are ridiculous and petty. I wrapped them, three small pictures, and the Ladies were to call for them at my house. You understand I was alone, then. I did not have my Lala and my Baba as I have now; I did not even have a houseboy, for I was—you must know it—even more hard pressed then than I am now. That was in fact my low point, my very lowest point—although perhaps I can see a lower one coming, now that Liliane died under my care." He stopped and looked at me beseechingly. I knew what he wanted, and I was already beginning to squirm. He looked at Miss Finney and said, "Doctor, would you prescribe for me just one ounce of whisky?"

Miss Finney smiled at him and said, "I couldn't do that, medically, without giving you a thorough examination. But socially, I must say you seem more comfortable *and* more fluent with a glass in your hand. Why not? Suppose I join you." She turned to me and said, "Hoopie, two whiskies. Short ounces—ice and water and a short ounce for flavoring." She said to Gollmer, "Think that's all right?"

Old Gollmer sighed happily, reached for his empty glass, and handed it to me. He began looking a little better even while I was mixing his drink. And I must say for him that he drank this one in tiny sips as if it were the last short ounce of whisky in the world.

"So I wrapped the pictures," he said, "and left them in my front room. But I left the house that afternoon, and on the door I pinned a note, saying that the pictures were wrapped and waiting just inside the door. Madame de St. Nicaise says that when she drove by to collect them, she sent her boy in to pick them up. He brought out the pictures I had intended, and the 'Venus' also." Our question was so obvious that we didn't even have to ask it. He paused for a moment and

149

then said, "Unfortunately, the 'Venus' was wrapped too."

"*That,*" Miss Finney said, "is too bad. How did it happen to be wrapped?"

"I always keep my pictures covered when the paint is wet," he said. "As a man living alone, I failed to keep my house very tidy, and the dust—"

"But you weren't working on the 'Venus.' You had finished it."

"I had finished it and varnished it. If you know oil painting, Dr. Finney," he said, "and especially oil painting with cheap paints and cheap canvas as I must do it, you know that the oil dies out dull and flat, especially over the corrected spots—and in this picture the corrections were very many indeed. But I had given it a coat of what is called retouching varnish, and on that the dust of my house would have settled and stuck in a thick coat. So the 'Venus' was varnished and then immediately and neatly wrapped. But it was put off to one side, and there, Dr. Finney, is what I *can* say, that it was perfectly obvious that the little pictures were ready and waiting, but to get the 'Venus,' it was necessary to enter the room and find it and take it from its place in the corner against the wall. But Madame de St. Nicaise forestalled me on that; you know her particular pet phrase, *ces indigènes.* Her stupid boy, she says, not only brought out the three little pictures, but in his stupidity saw the large wrapped picture and brought it also. Oh, according to her story, Madame de St. Nicaise would have given her own head to have kept the 'Venus' from being shown."

"Well, I see you can't make much rebuttal on that story. After all, if the boy was after wrapped pictures—"

Dr. Gollmer said quietly, "Oh, but I can."

"But you haven't."

"No. Because as I have said, it would only have made more trouble. But there is something I know, and I can tell you."

He paused long enough to select a starting point, and then said, "I came home that afternoon and noticed only that the little pictures had been collected. In the clutter of my room there was no reason to notice that the 'Venus' also was gone. I spent very little time in my house that day, and I spent that little time in my bedroom; I only passed through my living room. And that night, too, when I came home, I only passed through, and went into the bedroom. But the next morning when I went out, I heard about the affair at the auction the night before. Naturally I was horrified, and I went to my house immediately. And listen to me, Dr. Finney, and Mr. Tolliver—I tell you that every object in my house had been examined, and examined with care. Everything had been put back exactly in place, but in a house such as mine was then, one can see where the dust was disturbed. In my bedroom even *I* did some dusting, but I believe that it too had been entered, as well as the living room. I believe that my bureau drawers had been opened and their contents examined.

"Now that is not the work of a houseboy whose mistress is waiting impatiently in the heat outside, in her car. That was the work of Madame de St. Nicaise, who is a woman of morbid hatred, of morbid curiosity, a woman who, and I say this as a doctor to you, Dr. Finney—a woman who is sick with hatred and jealousy and frustration, deeply sick. I tell you that when I went through my house, alone that morning, I felt her there, and that my flesh crawled when I saw all the little signs of her lifting and examining things. Perhaps *I* grew morbid, Dr. Finney, but as I saw the signs of her all through that house, I began to imagine her there, fondling my fetishes, fingering my linen, and I could imagine the staleness of her body in the air, even that. And knowing that she had breathed in that room, it was almost as if I could hear it, the short, suppressed, excited breathing of the

151

snooper, and I tell you I could not take that air into my lungs, and I went out and sat on the steps of my porch, holding my head, and feeling my stomach turn.

"Then I began to think it out, and I began to be certain what had happened. I think that Madame de St. Nicaise dispatched the boy to my door while she waited in the car. Certainly she would never have entered the house in my presence, or even have set foot in my yard if I had been there. But I think the boy brought back to her the note, which he of course could not read. It told her that the house was empty. I think that then she looked around her; she saw how protected it is in my driveway; bushes and vines conceal everything, and nobody could see her enter the house. She got out of the car and perhaps went into the house with the boy, but I think she told the boy to wait. And then, in my house, she had a delightful time, spying on old Gollmer, poking into his things, hunting out the little intimacies. What she felt when she unwrapped the big picture in the corner, and saw the 'Venus' for the first time, you can imagine. Such triumph, such a beautiful feeling of evil discovery, such a full-born incredibly fortunate opportunity, ready-made, to disgrace old Gollmer and with him, Liliane. Because surely you know that she hated Liliane, although she would never openly speak one word against Morelli's wife, as she openly slanders me. Not that she refrained through loyalty, you understand— through self-interest. You say you saw her this morning. But what you have not seen is what I saw, before Liliane died, when I was in the house every day or several times a day, and could watch Madame de St. Nicaise while I also watched my patient. I tell you Madame de St. Nicaise is sick; she is very sick, sick with her body that no man has touched, and sick with her little ambition to be a great lady —she is love-sick and hate-sick. It is a kind of nymphomania of hate, and that is what she felt when she saw the 'Venus'— the excitement of approaching fulfillment, the discovery of the instrument for expressing her passion. Yes, I call it a passion. Both of us, Liliane and old Gollmer, in one stroke. I think she rewrapped the picture, and called the boy, and delivered the pictures to the hall."

Miss Finney murmured, "Of course, her boy could be questioned."

"Hah!" said Dr. Gollmer. "Naturally you do not believe that, not for an instant. In the affair of the cat, for instance, the word of my boy who brought the kid-gut counted for nothing, but Madame invited that the word of *her* boy should be accepted, to say that she had burned the string before I offered to have tests made on it. With Madame de St. Nicaise the word of the *indigène* is to be accepted or rejected as it suits her purpose. And in any case, this community could never solicit native testimony; it would be too dangerous a precedent. For that matter, if the testimony were given, Madame de St. Nicaise is capable of threatening her boy and dictating his testimony." He managed to smile and said, "Now I am talking like Madame de St. Nicaise, who says that old Gollmer's boy will say what he is told to say. No, there was nothing to do but let the matter lie. And what I believe, I believe only from knowing Madame de St. Nicaise, and from seeing that my house had been gone over, object by object."

"Your door was unlocked. Anybody could have done that during the day."

"Of course. I told you my position was indefensible. I told you I have not even tried to establish anything except that Liliane did not pose for the picture and that it was collected by mistake. But Madame de St. Nicaise says that I put the 'Venus,' wrapped, where the boy would see it; that I left the house so that the mistake might occur; that if it had not occurred at this auction, I would have seen to it that it occurred at a later one; that I was determined to have my revenge on her, after our quarrel about the cat, by disgracing the family. And you can imagine her, Dr. Finney, the way in which she would deny the possibility of Liliane's having posed for the picture, in such a way that it would be obvious to the listener that Madame de St. Nicaise really thought Liliane had posed, but was lying for the sake of the family honor. No, she had to have both of us, both at the same time."

"And you haven't told all this to anyone at all?"

"No one," he said, and stopped abruptly. Then he said, "Except Liliane."

"Liliane! When?"

"That is the answer to your question," he said, "as to why Liliane insisted on having me. I have told you that I liked her; I found her sweet and agreeable, always, always eager to give pleasure, and incapable of giving pain. And that she thought I had deceived her, that she should even think that perhaps I had exhibited the picture intentionally—that I could not tolerate. For that matter I *had* deceived her to some extent, in asking her to pose for the head, when I meant to use it as I did, even for my own pleasure only. When she left town, when she went to South Africa after the scandal of the auction, I wrote her a letter—"

"Where'd you get her address?" Miss Finney snapped out, although I wouldn't even have wondered.

"You are quick, Dr. Finney," Gollmer said. "I got it from Morelli."

"*Morelli!* But you didn't tell him all this?"

"I insisted to him that I had never intended the picture to be seen by anybody but myself. I told him what was the truth, that I wanted to apologize to Liliane for asking her to pose for the head, without telling her how I planned to use it."

"Well, for—and how did Morelli take all this?"

"At first, very angry. Then, very polite and reasonable."

154

"He did give you the address?"

"Yes, and I wrote Liliane."

"You apologized and so on. But did you tell her what you've told us about Madame de St. Nicaise?"

Gollmer looked extremely uncomfortable and said, "Dr. Finney, we all make mistakes. We all begin to feel sorry for ourselves. After this affair, I was ruined. Perhaps when I wrote Liliane—I was even tempted to tell it all to Morelli— I did hope that it would somehow come out through her, and that Madame de St. Nicaise would receive some of the humiliation and calumny which she deserved as much as I did—more than I did, of course. But primarily I wanted to clear myself in Liliane's eyes. I could not stand it that she should think of me as she must have done."

"And you did clear yourself."

"If I had waited only a couple of weeks, I need not have written the letter. That was the time when suddenly I went on the tour with the French anthropological expedition. It was a godsend. Among other things," he said half humorously, "it brought me Lala and Baba. I came back much rested, and even with a little money. I might have then been able to refrain from writing Liliane. But as it was, I had already written. And when Liliane came back, I saw her very briefly on the street."

He stopped here and turned to me. He said abruptly, "Do you think Liliane changed, Mr. Tolliver, while she was in South Africa?"

"Yes, some," I said.

"How? In what way?"

"Since you ask, in an important way, I think. I've been thinking a lot about her, lately. She was quieter, for one thing. I didn't see much of her, though. I've been away part of the time since she got back, and we somehow just didn't happen to go to the same places."

"That was because she went to so few places," Dr. Gollmer said. "And of course you heard the rumors about her."

"About what happened in South Africa?"

"Yes, of course. Well? Do you believe them?"

I said uncomfortably, "But Dr. Gollmer, you know how people always talked about Liliane. They were just the usual rumors—the usual kind that attached themselves to Liliane." I said to Miss Finney, "I haven't mentioned this to you. When we talked about Liliane I hadn't got to that part. Miss Finney was curious about Liliane, of course," I said to Dr. Gollmer, knowing I was doing all this rather messily, "and I've been—"

Dr. Gollmer said, "You say, 'the usual rumors that attached themselves to Liliane.' In other words, you heard she had had lovers down there—or, specifically, a lover. Did you believe it?"

I really squirmed. Because I had believed it. I believed it because Liliane seemed so changed. Not in looks—she was as bloomingly healthy, as pink-gold and ivory as ever, but she had lost something of the quality of naïveté, some of the almost childlike air of direct and curious and unselective interest in life which she had had before. I had imagined that she had had a love affair, not a sordid tumble in the sheets or an experimental investigation of amorous indulgence, but a real love affair, and I was glad. I think I felt all this because I had understood, up there on the platform at the Funa that day, how easily it might happen, how innocently it might happen, and how sweet it could be. And as a matter of fact I had hoped it was true, and I had felt it was true because of the change in Liliane. I had hoped it was true in spite of the fact that any love affair which doesn't have time to fade out into mediocrity and indifference is going to end in sadness, and I felt it was true because I felt some of this sadness in Liliane, and because, the time or two that I saw her, our meeting at the Funa seemed so far away, as if something more important had intervened for her, just as it had for me. And I think all of this should explain why, when Dr. Gollmer asked me, "Did you believe it?" I said, "No."

"Why not?" he asked.

"I just don't think she was—easy, the way one always heard."

Dr. Gollmer smiled. "I beg your pardon, young man," he said. "I did not mean to turn this into an inquisition. But I wanted to make a point here. It is about the technique of slander used by Madame de St. Nicaise. Where did these stories of Liliane's lovers originate? Do you know anyone— anyone at all who was in South Africa while Liliane was?"

"Yes. Jeanne, the daughter. Liliane went down there to put her in school."

Dr. Gollmer looked startled for a moment, but then he said, "We will disregard Jeanne. To suspect a child of eighteen—well, of course, it is a possibility, but in this case I think not. What I am getting at is that it was Madame de St. Nicaise who began these South African legends. On several occasions, even to old Gollmer, and as I have said, I hear less gossip than most people—on several occasions acquaintances would say to me, *You've heard about Liliane's affairs? In South Africa?* And I would say, *No.* Then I would be told—the vague rumor, the shadowy lover, the ambiguous misbehavior—but credible, always credible, of a body like Liliane's. I would say, *Where did you hear this?* The answer would be *Here* or *There*, but twice it was *Madame de St. Nicaise.* Mind you!"

"But she wouldn't!" I objected. "She's stupid, but not that stupid. She wouldn't circulate a rumor about Liliane. You just said, about the 'Venus,' she would always deny Liliane posed for it—" and then I saw light and said, "Oh, of course."

"Yes," said Gollmer. "The same. I would say to my

gossiping acquaintance, *What! From Madame de St. Nicaise herself!* and *Oh*, they would say, *of course she was denying it*. A fine way to start a rumor, Mr. Tolliver, a classic way. Invent it for yourself, then deny it—all virtue, all rectitude, all loyalty! That was always Madame de St. Nicaise—and all scheming, lies, evil."

As he spoke I could see a monstrous head of Madame de St. Nicaise, the eyes glittering, the lips retracted, then moving rapidly in the grimaces of speech, then the end of the tongue darting out and back.

I heard Miss Finney saying in a matter-of-fact voice, "We got off the track somewhere, Doctor. You said you saw Liliane on the street after she got back."

Dr. Gollmer took a deep breath, and I came up to the surface myself, shaking off the specter of Madame de St. Nicaise. "Yes," Dr. Gollmer said. "We spoke only a few words. She thanked me for the letter, and told me that she believed me. But whether she ever mentioned it to Madame de St. Nicaise, or to Morelli, I very much doubt. She was never one to make any trouble that could be avoided. But when she became ill, and insisted on having me, that is why. She wanted to do that much to re-establish me in the position I had lost through Madame de St. Nicaise and her slandering. Liliane," he said, "Liliane—" and he spoke with a kind of despair and humility "—I only hope it did not cost her her life."

"Nonsense," Miss Finney said. "You treated her the way practically any other doctor would have."

"I was too casual," he said. "Even this time, too casual."

But it wasn't Dr. Gollmer's casualness that Miss Finney and I were thinking about, and both of us knew it. We were all three silent for a while, but I knew for sure that Miss Finney had been thinking of Madame de St. Nicaise when she shivered a little and sat up straighter, with an air of finishing the interview, and said, "I knew that woman was stupid, and I knew she was malevolent. I haven't really learned anything new about her, except that she is everything I thought she was to a more intense degree. She used to make me just plain mad." She looked at Dr. Gollmer and said, "But now I think she scares me a little bit."

"You may take the word of old Gollmer, Dr. Finney, that she is something to be frightened of. Like many dangerous people, she appears only comic, or a little pathetic. But there is a rest home in Thysville, you certainly know—Dr. Chaubel's mental hospital called a rest home, and if Madame de St. Nicaise were my patient, I think she would go there for observation."

"I'd hate the job of getting her there," Miss Finney said. "Dr. Gollmer, you saw Morelli and Madame de St. Nicaise together while Liliane was ill. What do you think?"

Dr. Gollmer said, "What I think is what anybody who knows the history of that family should think, after one glimpse of Morelli and Madame de St. Nicaise together. I have said nothing about it, since I have always tried, this afternoon as always, to say nothing at all against Madame de St. Nicaise except where she was directly concerned with me, where she has directly sought to do me harm. But you have asked, and I will say this: that the woman is hopelessly enamored of Morelli, that she was probably hopelessly in love with him even when her sister was alive; that in Morelli now she has concentrated everything—the love she bore her sister, the desire she has always had for him, even the love she bears his daughter. And if she could marry him, and have the position in full recognition which she has filled for so long in half-measure—if she could stop being a kind of housekeeper, and become Madame Hector Morelli, established in her own home—if she could have that, she could have a life worth having. Her whole life centers in Morelli. Especially," he said, and he wasn't without a little satisfied malice here, "since the passing of poor Mimette."

"Yes," said Miss Finney. "And Morelli? What is she to him?"

"My dear Dr. Finney," Gollmer said, "to any man, especially to a man who has had a wife like Liliane, Madame de St. Nicaise could only be a rather dull and unlovely object which is not discarded because it has become indispensable around the house."

He rose now and said, "It is, of course, a great relief to me to have said these things at last." He said unnecessarily and a little pompously, "I hope you understand that it is a tribute to your integrity as a doctor and as a person." I had risen too, and he turned to me and took my hand. "Perhaps in a very small way, also, a tribute to your whisky, Mr. Tolliver, and certainly an acknowledgment of my belief in your discretion, as vouched for by Dr. Finney."

"Thanks," I said. We all moved toward the door, but just as we got there, Miss Finney said, "Oh, by the way, have you heard any rumors about Morelli and this new girl?"

"New girl!" he exclaimed. "No, none. What rumors?"

"Some girl in Thysville," Miss Finney said. "Well, you'll hear it soon. Things like that don't stagnate once they get started, and we've already heard it."

"You mean a serious affair?"

Miss Finney said, "Very serious—according to rumor. Marriage."

Dr. Gollmer stood with his hand on the door, and said, "I know Morelli well enough to disbelieve it. Something that is supposed to have gone on while Liliane was away?"

"Something that's been going on for quite a while, yes," Miss Finney said. "You haven't heard anything at all?"

"Nothing. Of course I hear a little less of that kind of thing than most people do. But I find it difficult to believe of Morelli."

"You do? Do you think other people will feel the same way?"

"My dear lady," Dr. Gollmer said, "we have already said that a discreditable rumor already has a healthy start in life by the simple advantage of its discreditableness. Of course people will believe it. Don't you?"

"I don't know Morelli."

"I know Morelli," Dr. Gollmer said, "and two minutes ago I said I didn't believe it. But even while I stand here, I find that I am changing my opinion of him to allow me to consider the possibility. You see?" He added, "I am also thinking of Madame de St. Nicaise. Since you apparently saw her this morning in fairly normal circumstances, I take it that she has not yet heard."

"It was obvious that she hadn't," Miss Finney said. "Quite the reverse."

Dr. Gollmer said, "I would not want to be Morelli, when she does hear."

"No," Miss Finney said, "and I wouldn't want to be Madame de St. Nicaise either."

Dr. Gollmer gave something like a laugh and said, "It is quite true that I have really told you nothing at all this afternoon."

"Maybe not, but you've established a lot that I suspected."

"Then I must go. Will I see you again before you leave?"

"Make it a point to," Miss Finney said. "I'll be around perhaps a couple of weeks."

"A couple of weeks." He said very suddenly, "I might leave before that time myself."

"You? When did this happen?"

"Just now," said Dr. Gollmer. "Or perhaps when I handed you back that letter."

"Well for goodness' sake," Miss Finney said. "You'll have to tell me more about it, when you know more yourself. Hoopie, do you think you could get your boy to take Dr. Gollmer home?"

I went over to the office and found that the car and the

driver were there, so I had the car brought around to the yard, and Miss Finney and I waved Dr. Gollmer off. The car bumped out into the street in low, growled and complained through an interval in second, and finally went off with its normal sounds of internal bickering in high, with David, our driver, weaving from curb to curb as was his custom. I said to Miss Finney, "What next?"

"Thysville," she said. "You ready?"

PART THREE

CHAPTER FOURTEEN

Thysville is an extraordinarily pretty little town, built on such precipitous hills that the first-floor windows of one house are likely to look down on the roof of the house next door. There are some spectacular views—not of extreme distances, but sort of mountain landscapes concentrated and reduced—and it is usually fresh and cool there in the evenings. The houses are simple, with lots of comfortable living-porches, and there are pretty good accommodations for transients, since people from Léopoldville and Matadi frequently come there for short rests. All over the place there are tremendous great clumps of bamboo, shooting fresh and green and frothy up into the air.

It's an easy ride from Léopoldville by car, if the road isn't so wet that you bog down in the mud, or so dry that you bog down in the sand. It was reported good, and Miss Finney and Miss Collins and I drove it without any trouble, getting there in time for supper on the cool open terrace of the hotel.

I was tired, because I had had a little less than four hours' sleep the night before, and it had been an eventful day, what with Madame de St. Nicaise in the morning, Dr. Gollmer in the afternoon, and the drive to Thysville after that. Tommy Slattery let us have the Dodge on the condition that we foot his taxi bill while we were gone, and we left David, the driver, behind because he understood enough English to be a nuisance and we wanted to be free to talk on the way. So I drove.

But as a matter of fact Miss Finney didn't talk much. She was worried about something that had happened during the interview with Gollmer, she said, and in addition she didn't know exactly what she hoped to accomplish in Thysville, except that she knew there was bound to be something there which would tell us one thing or another, if we could get hold of it.

"How do we get hold of it?" I asked.

"How have we got hold of things so far?" she asked. "We talk to people about other people. You know Morelli well enough to be pleasantly surprised if we bump into him, don't you?"

"Well enough, for instance, so that if we happened to meet on the street in Thysville I might suggest a drink or something."

"That's well enough for a beginning," Miss Finney said. "And I know Dr. Chaubel at the so-called rest home. We'll just have to take what comes."

If she had any plans beyond that, she wouldn't admit it, and as for what she hoped, all she would admit was that if you kept poking around enough with people who had past, present, or possible future connections with a case, and if you remembered every little thing, and kept it all tucked away inside your head until the pieces began to fall together properly, you were pretty sure to get somewhere.

One thing that made me sore was that she had told me she had to have half an hour with Emily before we started off, so I had to sit out in the car and wait while they went up to their room at the ABC to gather together a few things and to give Emily a chance to report on the leg work, whatever it was, that she had been assigned that afternoon while we were talking to Dr. Gollmer. When I asked Miss Finney about this—I said, "Well, how do you feel about Emmy's job?"—she said, "Emmy did a fine job. She's turning into a real technician."

"What does that mean?"

"Hoopie, you're bothersome as a fly. Why don't you be quiet?"

"We might as well have brought David along to do the driving," I said. "I have a perfect command of English and I haven't learned a goddam thing."

"What would you like to know, for instance?" Miss Finney asked.

"You know what I want to know. I want to know what you put Emmy up to."

Miss Finney thought about this a moment, then she said, "All right, I'll tell you. Emmy's been out counteracting the rumor that Morelli's got a girl in Thysville."

"That's he's got one, or that he plans to marry her?"

"Both."

"And what do you mean by 'counteract'?"

"I mean deny."

"You're out of your head," I told her. "You know perfectly well, and you've said it again and again, that denying a rumor's just an effective way of spreading it."

"I certainly do," Miss Finney said.

"That's exactly the way Madame de St. Nicaise spread rumors about Liliane."

"It certainly is."

"Well, then."

"The point is that Madame de St. Nicaise has been a dirty fighter all along the line," Miss Finney said. "So I got to thinking, maybe the way to get at this woman is the fire-with-fire idea, or dose-of-her-own-medicine, and so on. I figured that like most dirty fighters she's likely to be more vulnerable to her own methods of attack than to any others. You know how it is—stupid people who want to harm others try to hit where it would hurt them most themselves."

Emmy sighed. "She seemed so nice, at first," she said.

"So I propositioned Emmy," Miss Finney went on, "and

gave her a general idea of what the situation was, including a general idea of what her buddy Madame de St. Nicaise was really like, pump-organ or no pump-organ. Madame de St. Nicaise hadn't heard about Morelli's girl this morning, and I just wanted her to hear as soon as possible. Drop a bee like that in a bonnet like Madame de St. Nicaise's and you're likely to get something. So I sent Emmy out on this little expediting tour."

"I had the most re*ward*ing afternoon," Emily said happily. Then she looked at Miss Finney, and Miss Finney nodded and said, "Tell him about it," so Emily said, "Well, I told you about how I was sitting at the piano bench at the meeting of the Ladies' group, because I had been playing 'Onward Chris—' "

"Never mind how you got on the piano bench," Miss Finney said. "We remember that from this morning."

"Well, then," Emily said, "I told you I heard some of these ladies whispering and all. Remember? Well, today I went around to all the places where those ladies might be, and the other ladies that maybe hadn't heard yet. I went to each of the ice-cream shops, and I hope I *nev*er see another dish of ice cream in my life—raspberry, vanilla, and banana— and I even went to the Equatoriale and had a lemon squash"— she gave a slight hiccup at the memory—"and I dropped into dress shops and things, and altogether I had a very busy afternoon. And so one place and another I would see these ladies that belonged to the group, and sometimes they would have friends along, and I would say that I thought it was mean and scandalous that such things should be said about Mr. Morelli, and that I had it on the best authority, which I was not at liberty to divulge, that there was *noth*ing to the rumor at all—*noth*ing." She concluded primly: "I think I managed to do quite a bit of good."

Miss Finney regarded Emily with pride and said, "You know, I've worked with Emily for nearly thirty years, and

I've never before thought or breathed a suspicion that she was more dangerous than skimmed milk and distilled water."

"Well I like that!" Emily squeaked in outrage. "Skimmed milk!"

"When that rumor gets to Madame de St. Nicaise you can call yourself Little Dynamite," I said. "Now there's another question."

"Not now there isn't," Miss Finney said. She sighed heavily, and I saw that she was really tired and worried. "I don't mean to sound cross, Hoopie," she said, "but I've got to do a little worrying. I'm not a very good worrier, don't have a real talent for it, and I need quiet."

"I'll be quiet, but tell me what you're going to worry about."

"Gollmer."

"About Gollmer how?"

"About Gollmer giving that letter back to me. I really mean it, Hoop, I've got to think something out, and what I've got to think out," she said, "is whether I ought to drop this case right here, or try to go on with it."

That shut Emily and me both up, because we had never either of us heard anything like that before from Mary Finney. The three of us rode along for a long time without speaking. Fifteen minutes later Emily said suddenly, "*Skimmed milk! The idea!*" but that was the end of that conversation because now I was thinking about things too, and we rode along, with the atmosphere in the car a little depressed.

But after we got there, it was fine. Thysville was so pretty and so simple, and the evening was so cool, and we had such a good supper of tender white fish and French fries and an honest-to-God green salad and an ice—which Emily couldn't face—that I felt rested enough to go on with anything Mary Finney suggested. But what she suggested was bed, immediately, for one and all.

"But *Mary*, it's only eight o'clock!" Emily objected.

"Don't talk back to me," Miss Finney said. "You've had a taxing day. Go on."

"I'm not going to go up to bed and leave you here talking all night," Emily said. "I'll go if you'll make Hoopie go too."

"Come on," I said. I didn't bother to say good night to Miss Finney, but propelled Emmy away from the table and saw her to her room.

"Good night, Hoopie," she said. "I know you're going right back down there with Mary, so don't think you're getting away with anything."

I said, "Good night, Emmy," and went back down and found that Miss Finney had moved from the table over to an easy chair on one corner of the terrace. She sat there with her knees crossed, waggling one foot and watching it. When I came up she looked at me and said in mock surprise, "What, you here? Siddown," and I pulled up a chair.

"No bed for me yet," I said, "not after one taste of blood."

Miss Finney looked at me with a look that would have been blank if there hadn't been a little guarded suspicion showing through it, and said, "What in hell are you talking about, Hoop?"

"About how this afternoon I dug one answer—of sorts—out of you, about Emily's leg work, and you've got my appetite whetted."

"What is it this time?" she said, still looking blankish. "No guarantee, you understand."

"I want to know what the major fallacy was that you said Emmy and I were both of us making."

"Oh, that," said Miss Finney. "You know I said if you'd done everything I suggested, you'd be seeing a little clearer."

"Go ahead, what didn't I do?"

"You didn't look up blackwater fever. I'm going to take it back about seeing clearer, though. I only wish it were that simple. I asked you what you knew about blackwater and

170

you told me. Then I told you I wouldn't call you exactly an authority, but you had all the popular notions down, and suggested you look it up. Well, the popular notions, like most popular notions, happen to be all wrong. You don't get blackwater fever from too much quinine."

"You're crazy," I said, without conviction.

"I also told Emily she didn't follow my medical career very closely," Miss Finney went on. "The fact is, you'll find blackwater occurring where there's no malaria at all. Makes it sort of hard to regard blackwater as the result of malaria plus too much quinine. Fifteen years ago I tabulated every reported case of malaria and blackwater in the records of the Congo, Kenya, and South Africa, and the two diseases just plain aren't coextensive—that's the word—here, or anywhere else. I wasn't the only one working on it, other people were doing it other places, but anyhow I did the job here and I got damn good publication. That old quinine gag just doesn't hold."

I said meekly, "But that doesn't mean Madame de St. Nicaise didn't do exactly what Emily and I thought. It doesn't mean she didn't hold out on Liliane's regular quinine hoping for malaria. It doesn't mean she didn't lie to Gollmer thinking his dosage would turn it into blackwater."

"Of course it doesn't," Miss Finney said. "It doesn't mean that Madame de St. Nicaise didn't believe exactly the same popular notion both of you believed, and act on it. It doesn't mean that every time she gave Liliane the prescribed quinine she didn't give it to her with all the satisfaction she'd have got out of giving her poison. That's why I say she's a murderess in intent and in moral fact—and in her own conviction, for that matter. I'm just as convinced as you are that she was capable of an action like that. And I can imagine her absolute joy when Liliane asked for Gollmer. She thought Gollmer murdered her cat, and now with Liliane in her hands and a chance to make Gollmer appear responsible for her death, she really had something, something that made the affair of the 'Venus' look insignificant. I was glad to hear all that from Gollmer, though; what Madame de St. Nicaise did there was almost like a rehearsal for this thing. Oh, she must have felt pretty good. But she was under a delusion all the time."

"She may have been under a delusion, but Liliane did die."

Miss Finney hitched herself uncomfortably and said, "And Liliane shouldn't have. With the kind of health she had, she should have survived malaria and blackwater too—if it was blackwater. It's perfectly true that Gollmer's treatment should have been adequate under normal circumstances. At least," she added grimly enough, "if those records weren't falsified."

"Would you mind telling me exactly what those records showed?"

"Perfectly normal course for a serious attack of malaria— serious, but not with any indication that it could be expected to terminate fatally. It showed a perfectly normal progress with every indication, toward the end, that Liliane was getting better, up to the last two days, when—bango! she dies, with the usual symptoms of malaria, which overlap the symptoms of blackwater, plus the specific ones of blackwater itself."

"Rigor and black urine," I said.

"Yes," Miss Finney said. "That little bit of popular knowledge happens to be correct. And incidentally you might take note that Madame de St. Nicaise undoubtedly knew that, along with her misconceptions."

"Does that mean something?"

"Something obvious," she said irritably. "Forget it."

She wasn't like herself at all. She always had had a way of saying things that would have sounded harsh and jibing if you hadn't seen that she was half smiling at you all the time, or just covering up the natural timidity she always had in showing any kind of affection, but now she really sounded cross, and I had never heard her sound that way before.

I said, "I don't see why you're so discouraged on this case. It seems to me—well, I don't know. What *is* the matter?"

"Look, Hoop," she said. "Stop to think. Doesn't anything strike you as odd about Dr. Gollmer and that letter I wrote for him?"

"It struck me as a fairly large-sized gesture when he handed it back to you, when he wanted it so much."

"That's exactly the way he wanted it to strike us," Miss Finney said a little acidly. "Anything strike you when he said he hoped Liliane hadn't cost herself her own life when she insisted on having him?"

"I thought he seemed moved—really, deeply, sincerely moved."

"He was. No doubt about that. And I'm afraid now that he had every reason to be. Don't you remember all the excuses I made when I told him how I had written the letter?"

"Sure, you were pretty insistent about all the reservations you put in—that your statement depended entirely on the accuracy and completeness of the records."

"Well for goodness' sake then!" Miss Finney cried. "Can't you put one and one and one together?"

"Three," I said, but I said it very meekly and in apology, not for the weakness of the gag, but because that was all I could make of it. Miss Finney was kind enough to ignore it.

"Excuse me for being cross, Hoop," she said. "I've asked you for a lot of your time and now I'm beginning to be afraid I've just wasted it. Here's what I'm worried about. Look back and see how all this business started. Someone comes to me and says this strictly old she-bitch is whispering Gollmer to death and he wants my help. Gollmer shows me a bunch of records, graphs of temperature readings and so on, taken by the old she-thing herself, by Morelli, and by Gollmer. There were enough of his own readings there to eliminate the possibility of the others being falsified, since his were consistent with the rest.

"Well, I've always had a soft spot for old Gollmer in spite of everything. He's always looked down his nose at a lot of the fla-fla I've always looked down my own nose at, and that's a bond. He's an old goat but he's an engaging old goat, and he's always been an acceptable routine practitioner as routine practitioners go out here. So I begin to think maybe I can give him a break on this letter thing. But I never go into anything cold, so I come to you and ask about Madame Morelli in general. I admit I came with a bias in the direction of suspicion, because Gollmer had told me about the rumors Madame de St. Nicaise spread about Liliane. And the more you talked, the more I began to be convinced there was something wrong. It developed far beyond the idea of just establishing enough facts so I could give Gollmer the letter, and before I knew it I'd got all steamed up and here I was carrying on what amounted to a murder investigation and nobody had asked me to or anything. But that would still be fine, if I still felt I could trust Gollmer."

"You don't?"

"No. I do not. I'm sorry to say it, and I'm sorry to discover it, but I don't. Those three things you were just now able to add up, Hoop—look at them hard. That letter was professional life or death for Gollmer. He's not going to give it back as a gracious gesture. He gave it back to me for two reasons. One, that he had misrepresented something or other in those records, and two, that if he managed to fool me—quite aside from his conscience hurting him—somebody else knew the records were wrong in some way or other, and could have exposed him. The only person interested in exposing him would be Madame de St. Nicaise, or conceivably Morelli.

"So the only way I can add it up—well, wait a minute. Gollmer admitted he was 'maybe too casual' even on this case; he 'hoped Liliane didn't cause her own death when she insisted on having him'; he's deeply moved, personally moved, by her death, it's on his conscience; and at the last moment he was unwilling to take a chance on having to stick up for the accuracy and completeness of those records. It just means that somewhere they're all wrong. Somewhere they're badly wrong, and he knows it."

"But if you think there was foul play," I said, "couldn't that mean there was even fouler play?" I said it as respectfully and as carefully as I could, but she seemed to have gotten over her pique, and now she was really talking it over with me, not just explaining things impatiently.

"That's the hell of it," she said. "But on the other hand it leaves me without a point of departure. If the records are all wrong, it could just as easily mean that Liliane was a lot sicker than they showed. In other words, Madame de St. Nicaise's contention that Liliane died because of inadequate medical attention could be perfectly true, just as much justified by the records—*more* justified maybe—as our suspicion that Liliane died, somehow, because Madame de St. Nicaise wanted her to. It leaves me in an awful hole. The trouble is, I let myself in for this thing under a misconception, and now I'm in it deep and discover I didn't have any legitimate reason for beginning it at all. If those damn records don't mean anything, I haven't got a leg to stand on if anybody should ask me why I'm all of a sudden carrying on a murder investigation."

"Nobody knows you are."

"I sure hope nobody ever will."

"Anyway, you do have a leg to stand on. The way Madame de St. Nicaise hated Liliane, and the way she kept the quinine records and nursed her and everything else—"

"Listen, Hoop," said Miss Finney patiently, "every day somebody dies that somebody else is glad to see dead. But you can't accuse them of murder just for that. The happiest moment in Madame de St. Nicaise's life to date may have been the moment Liliane died, but if Gollmer's records don't mean anything, I'm out on one hell of a shaky limb."

I said with lame enough humor, "Maybe the old girl will up and confess."

Miss Finney looked at me and said firmly, "Now you listen to me, Hoop. No matter how sure we are that Madame de St. Nicaise wanted Liliane dead, and no matter how obvious it is that she had every opportunity to kill her, we haven't one single jot, tittle, or iota of proof of any kind. We never did have, if that's what you're going to tell me, but we at least had a bunch of records that said there was no reason Liliane should have died, that she wasn't sick enough to have died, that the treatment was the right treatment, and so on. Hence that she did die was some kind of indication— not a proof but an indication—of the strong possibility of foul play. *But* since I can't trust those records, I haven't got one single goddam thing I can point to, except what I know of human beings, to show why I think Liliane was murdered. And even if what I know about human beings is some kind of basis for me to work on, it's no kind of basis to make a charge on, and without one single lick of tangible evidence I'd probably be open to criminal investigation myself if this thing went beyond you and Emmy and me."

I said, "All right, you seem to be in an indefensible position. Just as a happy daydream, tell me what the ideal solution to your problem would be?"

"That's easy," Miss Finney said. "Ideally, I'd like to produce the murderer's voluntary confession without anybody knowing I'd ever even suspected murder, much less done anything about exposing it."

"Fine," I said. "Got any idea how to go about it?"

"Well," she said, a little grudgingly, "I guess you might as well know I *do* have some idea how to go about it." She paused a moment as if wondering whether to tell me, and then decided she would, and said, "In fact, we've already done quite a bit of work on it, quite a bit of work." I opened my mouth, but she said quickly, "I'm a vain woman, Hoopie, and at the moment I'm a slightly discouraged woman. If it works, I'll tell you about it. If it doesn't, I'd rather not. I'm at the point where I'm going to find I'm all wrong or all right, very soon now, and if you haven't *seen* what's been going on, then you can stay in the dark a little longer without its hurting you. But if I'm all wrong, I hope I learn it right away, because if I am, I've got to back out, and back out good and quick without stumbling."

"You're not going to be able to give up this case," I said. "If you do, you're Halfway Finney in my book from now on, and I never expect to see that day."

Miss Finney snorted at me in a way which I had learned to recognize as a demonstration of embarrassed affection, and said, "I didn't say I was giving it up. I said I was considering giving it up. I'm going to sleep on it. I'll sleep on it and see what happens. What I need is a break."

"What Madame de St. Nicaise needs is decapitation. Look at it that way. I've got one more thing to say."

"If it's anything but good night, I'm not listening," Miss Finney said. "For today I've had plenty and so have you."

"I just wanted to ask—"

"Good night, Hoop," she said, and rose and walked away. It was the first time she had ever really wanted to get rid of me and had resorted to anything worse than a little friendly kidding to do it, and I was so taken aback that I just sat there and watched her walk across the terrace. But at the door to the hotel she turned briefly and waved, and although I couldn't see the expression on her face in the shadow, I knew she was smiling, so it was all right.

It wasn't much past nine, but now that there wasn't anything to keep me up, I could hardly keep my eyes open long enough to get to my room. While I was undressing I wondered what kind of subterfuge I could use to maneuver an accidental meeting with Morelli and maybe get somthing from him that would cheer Miss Finney up, but I didn't get very far. The disturbing thought occurred to me for the first time that even Miss Finney had eventually to succumb to the hesitancies and debilities of old age, and I wondered if I had just seen the first crack in an edifice I had always thought of as impregnable. It worried me, but even so I must have gone to sleep the minute I lay down, because I certainly didn't hear the taxi drive up and then drive away, although even if I had, how would I have known that it was Miss Finney, still uncracked and impregnable, going out to do a little night work?

CHAPTER FIFTEEN

I woke up the next morning and knew right away that something was wrong. It took a couple of seconds to adjust to the strange bed and the strange room, but then I began to realize that what was really wrong was that the sun was high and nobody had waked me up. I looked at my watch and it was after nine. I had the awful feeling of lost time and of falling behind that you get when you oversleep, and by the time I had had a bath and a shave and got dressed, I began to have the feeling that I was never going to catch up.

But I could have saved myself the worry, because when I came charging down onto the terrace, Miss Finney and Emily Collins were sitting there as if they hadn't a care or a thought in the world. Miss Finney sat with her knees crossed, swinging one foot and watching it with a pleased air as if she found something particularly agreeable about the toe of her shoe, and Miss Collins was engaged in a pleasant reverie, chin in hand, looking out over the landscape that dropped off beyond the edge of the terrace.

We all said good morning, and Miss Finney added, "Better catch a little breakfast—we've had ours. Coffee's good this morning."

From the way she looked, everything in the world was good that morning, in a quiet way. I asked, "Any hurry?"

"Take your time," Miss Finney said. "Take all day."

"What—"

"Go eat your breakfast, boy. And I think I'd like another cup of coffee. Emily?"

"Me too," said Emily.

Miss Finney said, "Let's all have our second cups together. Have the waiter bring 'em over here, hmm?"

So I went and ate alone, then had the waiter bring a big pot of coffee and three cups over to where Miss Finney and Emily were sitting, and the three of us sat there like people who've gone somewhere for a vacation and haven't a thing to do with themselves except sit around and get fat.

I stood it as long as I could, then said, "What's new?"

"Nothing much."

"Oh." Long pause. "Well, what do we do this morning?"

"Sightsee, I guess. Might be pleasant. Think so?"

"Thysville can be exhaustively sightseen in thirty minutes."

"All right then, we'll sightsee for thirty minutes."

"What then?"

"Go home."

"Go *home!* Back to Léopoldville? But we haven't done anything here."

"Nothing to do for the moment. Things going all right, though."

"That's very odd," I said. "You must have slept on them awfully hard!"

"I went out last night for a little while," Miss Finney said. "Paid a late call. On Dr. Chaubel, at the rest home." She just plain stopped.

"That's treachery!" I said.

"Oh, no," said Miss Finney. "I hadn't planned to go out. I sent you and Emily to bed in good faith. But then when I got my shoes off I knew I was just going to lie awake all night if I didn't do something, so I put my shoes on again and left Emily there sleeping like a lamb and went to see Dr. Chaubel. Morelli was there."

When my exclamations had died away she said, "In a word, he came up here to Thysville to arrange with Dr.

180

Chaubel to take Madame de St. Nicaise into the rest home for observation—to put it politely. Chaubel gave me this big build-up to Morelli and when I let it escape accidentally-on-purpose that I knew Madame de St. Nicaise a little bit, they told me about this. That's all. Looks like I'm called in on the case. I've got my official standing."

"They asked you about Madame de St. Nicaise? What you thought?"

"Sure. And I told them. Told them I'd only talked to her once but noticed symptoms of emotional hypertension, instability, and some evidence of delusions of grandeur and persecution—all true. I didn't say anything about the sex angle. Morelli didn't mention it in so many words either, but you could see he was plenty aware of it. Puh-lenty. I wouldn't be surprised if the old girl had already propositioned him on the score of holy matrimony and that's what sent him here. If she hasn't actually propositioned him she sure has made it plain where her expectations lie. And that's enough to scare any man to death."

"Not grounds to commit a woman as a mental case, though. I could name a dozen—"

"No doubt. I didn't mean to imply he was putting it on those grounds."

"What about Morelli? What'd you think of him?"

"I didn't mind him at all. Sort of liked him. Felt sorry for him. Big puffy flabby pasty fellow—what did you call him? Rubens Hercules gone soft? He's a lot like that—must have been awfully good-looking in a red-faced way, once. Through with your coffee? Let's sightsee and get it over with."

We went to the car, where it had been standing at the curb all night, and started out at random. Sightseeing in Thysville simply means driving over all the available roads and looking at different perspectives of houses, hills, and clumps of bamboo—all very pleasant but not much to buy postcards of.

I said, "Now that you've seen him, you understand why I was so surprised when I heard Morelli had a girl here. Gollmer was too."

"He and Gollmer are about the same age, if that's your reference," Miss Finney said.

Emily muttered, "That nasty old Gollmer. And he has *two*." She muttered something else that sounded like "All that whisky" but I let it pass. Miss Finney didn't say anything to Emily or to me. We rode along in silence, and neither Miss Finney nor Emily gave any sign of expecting to break it.

I pointed out one of the frothy green geysers.

"Bamboo," I said.

"Thanks," said Miss Finney. In her part of the Kivu there are bamboo forests. With gorillas.

"Somebody had to say something," I said. "Know any word games? Want to sing songs? Recite?"

"I thought we were sightseeing," Miss Finney said. "Do we have to go yap yap yap all the time?"

"*I* do," I said, "or I never learn anything. Getting you to talk today is like building a fire under a mule."

"Go ahead, ask me something."

"That's easy. What about Morelli's girl? Any leads last night?"

"I mentioned her, that's all," Miss Finney said. "I sort of warned Morelli. I said if I didn't mention it, my conscience would hurt, and it would have, too. I said there was a rumor going around Léopoldville that he was keeping a girl in Thysville and planning to marry her. I said I wouldn't mention it to him if I thought it was important one way or another whether he had a girl or not, but I *did* think it was important for him to know people were talking about it, in case he didn't already know, because of the way Madame de St. Nicaise was likely to take it. I told him she hadn't heard yesterday morning but if she did hear it was going to constitute a significant factor in her attitude. Something like that. And if that doesn't tell him to watch his step, I'm sure I don't know what would."

"How did he act? Embarrassed?"

Miss Finney grinned. "He didn't even deny it," she said. "He was pleased as Punch to have it mentioned. He got a look on his face like a college sophomore who's just been told he ought to be in the movies. At his age and in his condition, it's a tribute. He was really eager to have me on this case," she added. "I let him beg me a little."

"That's all fine, except you're not going to need me any more. Now that you're officially on the case, medically, you can do your own unofficial ferreting. What do we do next?"

"They're planning to go to Léopoldville tomorrow morning," Miss Finney said. "I'll have to be there with them. We can go now, or poke around here for a while. What would you like, Hoopie?"

"Let's poke around here," I said, "until it's too late for me to get back to my desk today."

So we did.

CHAPTER SIXTEEN

Poking around one way and another, we managed to kill time until about noon. Then we admitted that the sooner we started back to Léopoldville, the happier we'd be. But we had to eat, since there wasn't any way to eat on the road back, and for variety we went to the other hotel, there being two in Thysville, and that was why we didn't get Dr. Chaubel's message earlier.

We weren't very hungry, but we ate too much anyhow, the way you always do when you're just marking time. When we started back to our hotel, Miss Finney asked me to go past Dr. Chaubel's so that she could say so long, and ask if there was anything she could do for him in Léopoldville.

Emmy and I waited outside in the car while Miss Finney went in, but she came out almost immediately. "Funny," she said, as she climbed back into the car. "He's already gone to Léopoldville himself—with Morelli. Let's go gather up our things and get started."

At our hotel there was a note waiting, written on the hotel notepaper:

Dear Dr. Finney, it said,

After further reflection on our conversation of last night, our friend M. is uneasy and has decided that the affair of the rumor concerning him is urgent. Hence we are leaving this morning in the hope of reaching the lady in question before she hears. We are sorry to miss you here but M. feels we must leave immediately in the hope of avoiding additional unpleasantness in Léopoldville. We will see you there as already arranged, for a more complete examination of the patient. *Chaubel*.

Just what Miss Finney thought when she got this note would be hard to say. She didn't change expression when she read it, but I do know this much: we had been very leisurely about our sightseeing and we had been very leisurely about eating a big lunch with a couple of leisurely cigarettes afterward, so that it was getting on toward two in the afternoon when we finally got Chaubel's note, but there was nothing leisurely at all in the way Miss Finney saw that our things got gathered together and our hotel bill got paid and we got started out on the road.

About getting stuck in the sand I don't even want to talk. I had become infected with Miss Finney's feeling of urgency, although she hadn't said a thing, and I was driving too fast. Also I suppose that the ease of the trip up had made me overconfident of the road. All I know is that I hit a bed of soft dry sand to one side that I would have avoided if I had had my wits about me, and it took us three mortal hours to get out of it. We had to wait until a car passed, and since they didn't have a rope or chain any more than we did, we had to wait while they went on to Thysville and told a truck to come back and pull us out. I will go into this much detail, though: it was hot. And I'll say that Miss Finney never gave any indication you could put your finger on that she was about to go wild, but she was, and you could sense it.

So it was well after dark when we finally drove up to the ABC. Without asking myself why, I came on into the lobby with Miss Finney and Emily. Miss Finney went directly to the telephone and called Morelli's house; she was still waiting for an answer when the desk clerk came across the lobby and handed her a slip of paper. Dr. Chaubel urgently needed Miss

Finney at the hospital, it said; he had called her in Thysville and been told she had left for Léopoldville.

Miss Finney said quickly to the clerk, "Know anything more about this?"

"No, Madame. It came in late this afternoon."

"Call 'em for me, will you? Say I'm on the way out there. Hoopie?"

We went tearing out to the car and nearly bisected little Emily in the door. "I'm *not* staying behind!" she cried. "Move over."

They were waiting for us at the hospital entrance, and an attendant began hurrying Miss Finney through the lobby and down a long corridor. Emily and I followed along behind; I had the sensation that we were attached to some fast-moving object so that we streamed out horizontally with our feet fluttering in the air.

"Who's the patient?" Miss Finney was saying.

"Monsieur Morelli."

"Bad?"

"Very bad, Dr. Finney. Dr. Chaubel is afraid there's no—"

"What is it?"

"Strychnine."

The attendant stopped at a door near the end of the corridor. He put his hand on the lever to open it for Miss Finney, then for the first time seemed really aware of Emily and me.

Miss Finney said briskly to the attendant, "Put 'em somewhere. Hoopie, Emily—wait for me."

The attendant opened the door and Miss Finney went in. I caught a glimpse of white walls and bright light before the door closed. The attendant looked at us hesitantly, made a decision, and motioned for us to follow. We went back along the hall, at a more reasonable pace now, and about halfway down the corridor the attendant stopped and opened a door for us.

Madame de St. Nicaise glanced up, a Madame de St. Nicaise most bizarrely altered in appearance. In a chair by her side was a stranger, a sturdy woman in her thirties, who looked up from the magazine she was reading and regarded us uncertainly. She almost spoke, but the attendant bowed slightly and closed the door behind Emily and me, leaving us standing there awkwardly. Madame de St. Nicaise might not have known us any more than the strange woman did, and was less interested in us.

"I'm sorry," this woman said, "I'm afraid the attendant made a mistake. This is a private waiting room." She indicated Madame de St. Nicaise with a glance of explanation.

"We know Madame de St. Nicaise," I said, but the sight of Madame de St. Nicaise in this condition was more shocking than the discovery of her corpse would have been. When I had last seen her she had been experimenting with lipstick. Now her whole face was elaborately made up—or recently had been. Her ordinarily dull flesh was like an old rag that had been in the wash with brightly colored garments which had faded on it. Here it had taken on a patch of blue, and there a blear of red. The remains of eye-shadow tinted her lids unevenly, mixed with sooty dark smudges of mascara. A few clots of mascara still adhered to her eyelashes, and her brows had been thickened and shaped inexpertly with mascara and pencil. Tears or perspiration had mixed these tones with the rouge on her cheeks; the rouge had been partially washed or rubbed away, but remained clotted in the wrinkles so that they stood out like nets of small blood vessels. Her mouth presented a disturbing effect of double exposure; without reference to the shape of her own pallid lips, she had designed over them the silly, pursed, rosebud mouth that was fashionable in the twenties, and her entire face, but not her neck, had been dusted with what looked like white talcum. On top of this scarecrow mask her hair, which I had always seen agreeably parted in the center and drawn back into a knot, had been tortured and burnt into uneven waves and kinks. Some strands remained straight, while others were hunched and twisted, and here and there the scorched, dried end of a lock protruded stiffly from the mass.

She made no sign of recognition, although she kept looking at me as if she half-recognized me from time to time in between periods of wandering. I stood it as long as I could, then nodded to her, and she nodded back, with an automatic smile twitching her lips for a moment before they fell lax again.

The stranger beside her said to me, "Then you are a friend of Madame's, Monsieur?"

"Yes, we are—old acquaintances."

Emily nudged me and I turned to her stricken face. "I can't stay here, Hoopie," she whispered. "I'm going out. I'll be in the car or somewhere." I got up and opened the door for her. "Buck up," I managed to say just as she went out, but she couldn't answer. She gave me that stricken look again, and then turned and started down the hall. I closed the door and sat down again, opposite Madame de St. Nicaise and her companion.

"I'm not certain you're supposed to be here," the woman said, doubtfully. She gave ever so quick and meaningful a glance at Madame de St. Nicaise, and I placed her for the first time as probably someone connected with Dr. Chaubel. She hissed at me suddenly; I realized that she had whispered, "*Shock*." She said in a natural tone, "Madame and I are waiting for news of her brother-in-law."

"Yes," I said. "I know Monsieur Morelli."

Madame de St. Nicaise turned her face to me and gazed from it in a way which I can only call slow. Her glance seemed to reach from her eyes to mine at an infinitely slow pace. I thought she might speak then, but soon she drew her eyes away and turned instead to the woman. She said in a very slow voice that I wouldn't have recognized as hers, "Is . . . he . . . dead . . . yet? I . . . want . . . to . . . say . . . it."

"It's all right, dear," the woman said professionally. "We mustn't give up hope."

She took Madame de St. Nicaise's hand and patted it, but Madame de St. Nicaise withdrew it and said, still slowly, "No—he will die. He said to me, *I cannot stand it;* that is when he took the poison. If he wants to die—he will die."

"There, there," said the woman.

"But I want to say it," Madame de St. Nicaise insisted. "Hector will die, then I want to say it."

"I know, dear. You told Dr. Chaubel."

"No one believes me," said Madame de St. Nicaise. "It must be taken down. Where is the paper and pencil?" She began twisting her fingers together, and her voice rose. "*Where is it?*" she wailed. "I *will* have it! If I don't say it, I will forget it!"

The woman looked at me a little desperately and said, "There, there, the young man will get it. Could you possibly go to the office and ask for pencil and paper?" She flicked a glance in the direction of Madame de St. Nicaise and pursed her lips and raised her eyebrows at me.

"Glad to," I said. When I reached the door, Madame de St. Nicaise said anxiously, "Come back! You'll come back? Because I have it all straight, and they are trying to confuse me. I must, I must say it!"

"Don't worry. I'll be back."

I went on down the hall to the offices, which radiated off the circular lobby, and got a big stack of paper and some pencils. I don't know at what point I decided I might really be going to use them; I know that I was already excited at the idea when I started back across the lobby and entered the long corridor. At the far end of it I saw a hillocky silhouette that could be only one person. Miss Finney and I advanced toward each other, and when I could distinguish her face I saw it was pretty grim.

We met and I said, "How is it?"

"I was too late. Nothing to do."

"Then Madame de St. Nicaise wants to make a—"

"Statement. I know. Chaubel told me. Can you really take it down?" she asked, looking at the paper and pencils. "We might be able to find a secretary or something."

"I do stuff for Tommy Slattery all the time. I can do this."

"I'll go in with you. If I seem to disturb her too much I'll go out."

"She's more apt to disturb you," I said. "Wait till you see her."

"You should have seen poor Morelli. The way I feel about Madame de St. Nicaise right now, no way she looks could bother me," Miss Finney said.

"I'm afraid to tell her Morelli's dead," I said. "She keeps saying he's going to die but how do we know she won't crack when she hears it?"

Miss Finney looked at me hard for a moment. Then she said, "We've got to get that statement no matter how we get it. Just go in there and say you're ready for it. If you have to say he's dead, take a chance on it. Do you think you can do this alone, Hoop?"

"Why? Aren't you coming in?"

"Changed my mind. Madame de St. Nicaise didn't exactly fall for me."

"She hardly seems to recognize anybody."

"But she's in a talking mood. I don't want to take a chance. That woman in there's from Dr. Chaubel's. She and Emmy can witness your report. I hate to miss it."

"Emmy's gone."

"Damn!" said Miss Finney. "Look—I'll stand outside the door. I'll keep my foot in it. If you need me, I'll know it. Go on in, Hoop, before she changes her mind."

We had been talking very low, a few doors away from the waiting room. Now we went to the door and I went in. The door closed behind me but I saw the open crack. Madame de St. Nicaise fixed her gaze on me and half rose from her chair. She glanced down at the paper and pencils in my hand, and sank back. The two women looked at me, each of them asking with her look the most terrible question of all: *life or death?*, the stranger with mild curiosity, and Madame de St. Nicaise with hope, but not, I knew, for life.

I said, "You may make your statement now, Madame." I could as safely have said it flatly, "Morelli is dead," because Madame de St. Nicaise accepted it, and simply spoke his name three times: "Hector . . . Hector . . . Hector . . ." It is a name with contemporary associations of the vaguely comical, the comically grandiose, but as Madame de St. Nicaise spoke it the first time it was tremendously moving, full of loss and sadness. But when she spoke it the second time, almost immediately, she spoke it in puzzlement and confusion; the third time, she spoke it in dismissal. It was a thumbnail history of a love affair, and then Madame de St. Nicaise began talking without any further preliminaries, so that I had written the first half-dozen words before I had sat down. It was easy enough to get; except for brief passages of nervous uncertainty, and an occasional phrase spoken in excitement, she spoke in the slow, monotonous, inward-looking voice she had used when I first came into the room.

"*I am Madame de St. Nicaise, you know,*" she began . . .

"I am Madame de St. Nicaise, you know, Hélène de St. Nicaise. Helen of Troy was the most beautiful woman in the world. It is very odd that I have never married. I have been very much loved. But of course I loved my sister very much. My sister Jeanne. She married the man who has just died. You know him. Hector Morelli. Sometimes I think the natives did it—the things that happened to me, to Hector. The way he married that peasant, Liliane. He wanted me.

191

My sister Jeanne died, you know. Then Hector wanted me. That was perfectly natural. But he married Liliane. The natives can do things like that, they can make it happen, they have ways. They do it with—you know. Bad things."

Her face took on an expression of enormous guile; she turned her head slightly to one side and looked at me from the corners of her eyes. Then quite suddenly she turned straight to me again, and her face relaxed into lines of terrible weariness.

"I have been through so much lately. I want to tell about it. Now that Hector is dead. While Hector was alive, I couldn't. While he was alive I couldn't tell about the pillow. But now he is dead, I must tell about it. Otherwise people might think I was bad. But I have always been good."

She paused and seemed to look to me for corroboration. I managed to smile, but it felt as if my lips were shriveling. She returned the smile, but it faded, and her eyes wandered past me and into the empty corners of the room.

"Even the things I did," she said, "you know, some of the little things I couldn't tell people about—those were really good, because they were for Hector. I am sorry that Hector was bad. Toward the end he was very bad, he did a bad thing. Do you think it helps for one person to confess for another? I hope so, because that is what I am doing. I want to confess for Hector. I saw him do it. It was terrible, of course—a terrible thing to do. When I saw him doing it, I said, *Oh, it is bad, bad*—and yet I knew he was doing it for me, because he wanted me. You know, it is a shame it wasn't me from the beginning. But I did love my sister. Now it will never be me. Poor Hector."

She paused now, in concentration, yet she spoke without horror or fear as she said, "I came into the room, and the pillow was still over her face. She was so much better, and he thought I was out of the house for the afternoon and he had told the boys they must leave the house because Liliane was so much worse." She looked at me again, and said almost gaily for a moment, "I happen to know he told them that. Oh, I have ways!

"The quinine didn't work. That was Gollmer's fault. He calls himself a doctor! That was really funny, almost. I used to laugh about it. I would say to myself that Liliane hadn't had her quinine for so long, not for so very long. It is no wonder that she—you know, malaria. I couldn't help that. I put it on our daily chart every day. A little mark every day. Oh, I kept a very good house for Hector, nobody ever kept a better, all of us had little marks every day on the chart. For quinine. We wouldn't want any irregularity in the records so I put down all the marks. But what a fool old Gollmer is. He ruined it all. He was already a murderer, you know; I called him a murderer in public, before everybody, after the concert. Some people laughed at me for that, how silly of them, because he was. You see?

"But Gollmer is really a fool, if he had known how much quinine to give Liliane, of course it would have been bad, it would really have turned into blackwater. I showed him all the little marks—all that is quinine, I said, ten grains a day, ten grains for each little mark. And he prescribed quinine for the malaria. And she kept getting better. If he had known what he was about she would have grown worse. Do you understand that? I did. It seems very odd now. It works several ways. And he calls himself a doctor.

"But that doesn't count now. Have I told you about finding him there with the pillow? Pressing it down so hard. Not Gollmer." She was very quiet for a moment, then she said as if surprised, "Hector! But I said to everyone that Gollmer was a murderer. I have said so, over and over again, I have told everybody. He is no better than a murderer, I have said, over and over again. If it weren't for him, Liliane would be alive today, I have said. It isn't true but it pays him back for Mimette so that makes it all right. Don't you think so? They could have hanged him for Mimette, if the law was what it should be. There ought to be some reform.

"The pillow was still over her face. And I said, *Hector, Hector, what what have you done, you have killed Liliane,* and he said, *Yes, for her adulteries.* He said that, not I. I never mentioned her adulteries, not once. Never. And then we did so many things. I was wrong, wasn't I? To help Hector? But how could I tell. The scandal, he said. Hide it, he said, no one must know. In our family, a family like ours, the scandal. And Liliane, only a peasant, a family like ours, and when Gollmer finally came he was so drunk he was easy to fool, and after two days of not seeing her, only our records to show, and we fixed those up. Burn the bed sheet, it was so black, so discolored, say it was, only say so. Gollmer is drunk, he will never admit. Rigors, too. Say rigors. Hector was so silly, he cried so much. But we fixed it to fool Gollmer. If the law were right they would hang him.

"The pillow was still over her face. It was there for so long. Excuse me, sometimes I have to stop and think; I have to get it straight. Yes, that was it, I came in and he was there, holding the pillow over her face. I think he gave her some sleeping pills with her medicine first. Did he tell me that? I have ways of knowing these things; I don't know whether I should tell you about them or not. The sleeping pills would have been a good idea. Do you know, I had even thought, myself—but then, that is so difficult, because you don't know how many, too many and they get sick and lose them, not enough and they don't die. But a good idea. Of course she had been very sick and she was weak but she was getting better and they struggle when you put the pillow on their face. The pills would help. Did I only wonder about it or did he think of it? No matter now. Hector saved me. That is queer because I wanted to save Hector. That was just this afternoon, before we came here, that I wanted to save

Hector. Of course Hector would want me instead of her. So the pillow.

"Of course that is why we are all here now, because something happened. Just the way it happened before. Jeanne died and he married Liliane when he wanted me. Then all those years with Liliane, we must forgive him a great deal. Everyone knows what she was. I won't speak ill of the dead. And Hector never touched me, all those years. Then he put the pillow over Liliane's face because she was getting well, but it happened again. He came home this afternoon. I was waiting. They had told me about it this morning. Another girl. How could it happen again, I wondered, the natives do it, you know, they have ways, nasty ways. I think Gollmer is in with them. His house is full of nasty things, I have seen them, oh, I know!

"They told me. They said they thought I ought to know. Then they went away. So I thought, I must save Hector. It was a bad time; I sent the boys away, I told them not to come back. It was a very bad time. Toward the end of it I decided what to do, and I spent it making myself—you know, a little younger. You see?"

(She touched her scorched hair and smiled. "This is the way Jeanne did her hair, Jeanne, my sister," she said; she put one finger tip delicately to an eyebrow, and smiled. She put one finger before her distorted mouth, like an admonition to silence.)

"But when he came in, it was terrible. It was too late to save him, as it turned out. Oh, he laughed, he laughed! He said to me, *Hélène, Hélène, what have you been doing to yourself?* laughing, but he stopped laughing, and began saying things which were dreadful, although he thought they were kind. I was too late to save him. But I told him, I told him it must not happen again with this girl the way it happened with Liliane, and he denied everything, he said there was no girl. I thought for a moment I had saved him but then I found it was too late, I could not save him, because I was happy and I threw my arms around him. That was all right, don't you think? because it was what he really wanted, and I would have kissed him, I tried, I held him and I was trying to save him, if I could have kissed him I could have saved him, but I couldn't, and my wrists hurt and I was on the floor crying, crying, lying there crying, and then I remembered the whisky. I have ways, you know, I had fixed the whisky with the poison in it we had for the rats, it was strychnine, and I went and got it for him. He was telephoning, you know, calling Dr. Chaubel, as if I didn't know what that meant, so I got the whisky, and gave him some. *No, no!*" (she cried out, and wrung her hands distractedly, looking about her in confusion), "No, it was not that way, I am telling it wrong. I had it all straight but now I am forgetting it. Let me think. Let me stop to think! I must not let them know I gave him the whisky while we were waiting! I didn't let them know it, did I? No, he did it, I said to him, *Why do you want to be alive, to live again as you lived with Liliane?* I said, *Cuckold! Cuckold!* I said, *Cuckold and murderer, you killed Liliane with the pillow, I saw!* and he said, *I cannot stand it!* and that was when he went out to the kitchen where he had the poison hidden, and took it. How could I know what was happening? What could I do? Nothing is my fault! I did little things I must not tell about, but Hector is already dead, everything is paid for now, and now you must let me go, *let me go, let me GO! GO! GO!*"

The woman, Dr. Chaubel's assistant, was very skillful. She produced the hypodermic and administered it to Madame de St. Nicaise almost before I knew what was happening. Madame de St. Nicaise began to grow quiet immediately, and she paid no attention when Miss Finney came in, followed by Dr. Chaubel. Dr. Chaubel said to me, "Morelli is safe now. He will be able to tell us everything, in the morning."

Madame de St. Nicaise turned her gaze on him half comprehendingly. Miss Finney said, "I don't think he'll be able to tell us much we don't know. Madame de St. Nicaise has given us a voluntary confession—in a way." In a moment she added, "Doctor, do you mind if Madame de St. Nicaise sees Morelli?"

"If she wants to. He's asleep, of course."

"It's that I want her to."

Dr. Chaubel said to the woman, "Will you bring Madame?" Miss Finney nodded to me, and we all went down the hall in the direction of the room where I had seen the bright light and the white wall. I looked accusingly at Miss Finney and she muttered, "Sorry. I had to fool you, Hoop. I knew she wouldn't say it unless she thought Morelli was dead, and you're such a poor dissembler."

We came to the door and went in. The room was dimmed now. Morelli lay there with his eyes closed in a face that was deathly haggard, but you could see his regular breathing.

Madame de St. Nicaise approached the bed and looked at him quietly. Dr. Chaubel and the woman were tense at each side of her, but she made no motion toward Morelli. In the dim light of the room her grotesque face was partially obscured, and as she stood there it was possible to feel sorry for her almost without horror of her. She stood so for a long time.

"How quietly he breathes," she said at last. Then, "Like Liliane. If I had a pillow again, now—a pillow . . ."

CHAPTER SEVENTEEN

Morelli corroborated the statement of Madame de St. Nicaise as it was translatable through her distortions and confusions. It was true that he had expected to be out of the house all that day. He had not been to the *Appro* offices during all the time of Liliane's critical illness, but once there, in spite of Liliane's great improvement, he had been uneasy enough—and exhausted enough—to return home early in the afternoon. When he opened the door of his house, it was unnaturally quiet; there were no boys anywhere, which was unheard of, and he had shouted out, and received no answer. He had run up the stairs and flung open the door to Liliane's room, making no effort at quiet. He saw Madame de St. Nicaise's back, bent over the bed, arms rigid, pressing downward. He said that she had no idea how long she had been that way; she was quite rigid, and as if numb, when he pulled her away. Liliane was dead, and from the flattened hair and the distortion of the face, the pillow must have been pressed there for a very long time before he arrived. It was probable that Liliane was in a stupor from the pills before Madame de St. Nicaise smothered her with the pillow.

Gollmer of course never knew anything of all this, and he shows up so badly, in any case, that I think it is important to bear in mind that he never had any suspicion that Liliane died as the result of anything other than his own carelessness and inefficiency—which were terrible enough but, in truth, would not have caused her death. He had been, as Madame de St. Nicaise had said, quite drunk by the time Morelli had located him and managed to convince him that he must come to the house. It had even been necessary to sober him up. All in all, Liliane's death was not reported until something like eight or even ten hours after it had occurred. When all this came out, Gollmer's license was revoked, but since he had reported the death as soon as he was mentally and physically able to do so, and since he had reported the cause of death as what, in good faith, he believed it to be, he was not guilty of a criminal offense.

For Morelli it was more serious. He pleaded that the shock of Liliane's death and the realization of Madame de St. Nicaise's condition, combined with his state of extreme fatigue, rendered him emotionally incapable of dealing clearsightedly with the situation, and he had fallen into the deception. He pointed out that as soon as he felt able he had gone to Dr. Chaubel as the first step in rectifying his mistakes, but Morelli's respect for conventional appearances was strong, and it is anybody's guess as to whether or not he would have revealed the exact circumstances of Liliane's death since it had become apparent, until Miss Finney's intrusion into things, that he would not have to do so. He was given a suspended sentence and I believe is in Belgium.

Madame de St. Nicaise is in Belgium too. She gives no trouble to the asylum attendants and spends many hours caring for her cello, upon which she refuses, they say, to put any strings at all.

CHAPTER EIGHTEEN

One afternoon, not quite two weeks after the events in the hospital, I was having coffee with Schmitty at the Equatoriale because it wasn't quite time yet for me to go and have lemonades, by appointment, with Miss Finney and Miss Collins at the ABC.

I said to Schmitty, "I don't suppose you'd be willing to confess as yet to having had an extremely unaccustomed attack of tender heart recently?"

"Certainly not," said Schmitty.

"I didn't think you would," I said, "but I wish you'd trust me, old man. I've had the same thing happen to me, lots of times."

Schmitty looked at me suspiciously and said, "Come clean."

"What I mean is," I said, "you wouldn't have been above going to a certain prominent female lady missionary doctor and suggesting that she make a belated effort to pull a fellow M.D. out of a hole, would you? Belated and, as it proved, somewhat misguided."

For lack of anything better to say, Schmitty used on me his favorite unprintable epithet that he saved for very special occasions.

"Who, me?" I said. "Same goes back on you again double. You did, didn't you?"

"What makes you think so?"

"I know Madame de St. Nicaise used to get in your hair." I looked at his scalp and added, "So to speak."

"You leave my hair out of this!" Schmitty barked, off

guard. He pulled himself together and said, "Anyway, she used to get in everybody's hair. She sure got in yours."

"Yeah," I said. "However, you were person number one in Léopoldville to pay cash down direct to the old boy himself for an original Gollmer, and I think it was a soft heart."

Schmitty shrugged unconvincingly. "What if I did?" he said. "What if I did go to Dr. Finney with a damn fool suggestion? Nothing happened."

I thought that someday I must tell Schmitty about everything that had happened as a result, but for the time being it would be better if nobody at all knew about it. Schmitty was muttering, "Get old von Schmidt mixed up in anything, it's jinxed from the start. What if I did?"

"Nothing," I said. "Nothing at all." I considered saying something else, such as that I, for one, would give him my unqualified personal O.K. any time, but if I had said it he would have been embarrassed every time he saw me from then on, so I let it ride.

Instead I said, "Absolutely nothing at all. Now if you'll excuse me, I have a rendezvous."

"I hope you get plowed under," said Schmitty ambiguously, and I left him.

Fifteen minutes later, over lemonades with Miss Finney and Miss Collins on the little section of balcony, overlooking the river, that went off their room at the ABC, we were talking along about nothing much, when I said to Miss Finney, "You were awfully lucky on this case, when you come right down to it. If Morelli hadn't turned up with that girl in Thysville you'd never have cracked it."

"You really think that?"

"Well, maybe you would have found another way, but as it was, this was pretty fortunate. Do you think he really had a girl over there?"

Miss Finney said, "Emily, what do you think?"

Emily looked from Miss Finney to me and back again and made small sounds of alarm.

Miss Finney laughed. "There never was a girl in Thysville," she said. "Emmy and I knew it all the time. It was just a rumor."

"And what makes you so sure of *that*? Just because Morelli looked sort of run down—"

"But Hoopie dear," Miss Finney said, "there never was a rumor, even, until Emmy went out to deny it. I told you once, when you asked me what kind of villainy I'd set Emmy about, that it was something you almost suggested yourself. And you did, when you said something about dropping rumors around town and seeing which ones came out ahead. So I thought shucks, with rumors as easy to drop as they are, why not set them about a little good work for a change? So I figured I'd drop this one about Morelli, and if Madame de St. Nicaise wasn't guilty of doing what we thought she had done, for the reason we thought she had done it, she might be uncomfortable—might itch a little bit or something—but if she *was* guilty, I knew it'd drive her wild. What's the matter?"

"Just shuddering, that's all. I don't suppose you thought about Morelli when you had this big idea? I don't mean to strike too high a moral tone in loose company, but I'd like to know if you even gave him a thought."

"Morelli's reputation, you mean. I thought of it. At the risk of sounding a little cynical, I'd like to point out what you very well know, to wit, that socio-sexual attitudes being what they are, a man's extracurricular affairs are apt to redound to his credit, no matter what the nominal moral attitude may be. As a corollary, the adulterer's activities redound to the discredit of his wife only; the adulteress's affairs redound to her own discredit as well as her husband's. That's called the double standard—maybe you've heard of it. Either way, it's tough on the girls."

"I suppose you picked up this quaint old attitude in Fort Scott, Kansas?"

"All right then, it's more a European attitude than an American one, but we're among Europeans. To suggest that a man in his fifties who already has a beautiful wife also has the attraction and the physical stamina to keep a second ménage going near by may be a scandalous suggestion on the face of it but at bottom what you're really doing is feeling his biceps and saying what-a-man. No, I didn't worry about Morelli. In passing, Hoops, I'd like to point out to you that if you had checked up on time sequences you'd have known it was an invention. Emmy mentioned it at breakfast that morning and I didn't have time to get to her and arrange for her to go around denying the rumor before she began on the job."

"The Ladies were already talking about it. Emmy said so."

"Oh, dear," Emmy said, appalled at herself in retrospect.

"Now, Emily," said Miss Finney, "keep your conscience under control. It all worked out, didn't it, just the way I said it would?"

"That's pragmatism," I said, "and I've been taught that pragmatism's naughty. The devil's methods in the Lord's work. But let that pass. I still say the Ladies had already been talking about it."

"But Hoopie—don't you remember how Emily was afraid to go out on the job, and I told her she had done just fine on Hoopie that morning, and you wanted to know what she had done just fine on you with, or something like that? *That* was the story about the Ladies. Of *course* they hadn't been talking about it. Emily and I had only invented it in bed the night before we had breakfast with you. I told Emmy what I suspected of Madame de St. Nicaise and how I thought we could get at her with her own methods, and Emmy agreed, but she didn't think she was up to the job—said she hadn't any talent for acting or deception, and I said she might try it out first where it would be safe if it failed—on you, Hoopie dear. So after breakfast that morning she gave you this long line of chatter about sitting on the piano bench playing 'Onward—' "

Emily interjected, "I *did* sit on the piano bench and I *did* play 'Onw—' "

"But she didn't hear any gossip," Miss Finney said. "She just made up that story."

"You can act, all right," I said to Emily. She gave me a pleading glance. I said, "I'll return your hook, line, and sinker if they ever turn up. In other words, there never was so much as a whisper of anything about Morelli and a girl in Thysville until Emmy went out and got bloated on banana ice cream and lemon squash and denied it right and left to the Ladies who were most likely to get it back to Madame de St. Nicaise quickest."

"Correct," said Miss Finney.

"I can only say," I told them, "that for the first time I am reconciled to staying here while you two take off for the Kivu. In fact I like the idea. Nobody's safe while you're around."

"Oh, *Hoop*ie!" Emily quavered, and I had to assure her that I didn't mean a word of it.

We talked around a bit and I was just getting ready to leave when a boy came up and said there was a gentleman in the lobby to see Miss Finney. Mr. Gollmer.

"Send him up," Miss Finney said. Everyone had heard that Gollmer was leaving town, even before his license was revoked. All they knew was that he was going across the river to Brazzaville, then by rail to Pointe Noire, and then by boat to Marseille. Everyone had tried hard to learn something more, but that was as far as they could get.

"Coming to say good-by, I suppose," Miss Finney said. It was past five o'clock already, and the last launch to Brazzaville crossed at six, from the station only a block or so away from the hotel.

Emily said in her wispy little voice, "Mary, should I leave?"

"Stick around," Miss Finney said, making Emily feel like one of the boys. "Hoop, go in and get another chair and bring it out here."

But when Gollmer came, he remained standing, because he said he had only a minute. Mademoiselle Lala and Mademoiselle Baba were downstairs waiting for him in the lobby, watching the luggage.

"Have them come up," Miss Finney said.

"Oh, no," Gollmer said, smiling, "they will be happier down there. They are always happier together than with other people."

"O.K.," said Miss Finney. "Well, we'll miss you, Gollmer."

Gollmer shook his head, still smiling a little bit. "No, I think not," he said. "Perhaps you, Dr. Finney, for you like people, but most of them—no, old Gollmer will not be missed, except as something to talk about. They have so little. And he leaves in disgrace."

He paused, and looked with a touch of uncertainty at Emily, and then looked at Miss Finney again and said, "I have come to give you the rest of Gollmer's story, the rest of the life of once-Doctor Gollmer." He chuckled, and said, "Old Gollmer is a *macareau* from now on. Yes, after so long a time, old Gollmer winds up a *macareau*."

"Dear me," said Miss Finney. "Well, at our age it's an easier life than doctoring. Do you want to tell me about it?" She added, "Don't mind Hoopie and Emily."

Gollmer chuckled again and said, "You see, I can not make a go of it here any longer, there is no point in trying to fool myself on that score. And Mademoiselle Baba has an elder sister in Marseille who has a successful—establishment, and we have had the most cordial letter from her, in response to one from Baba, saying that there are places for her and Mademoiselle Lala in it." He paused long enough to get over a slight hump of embarrassment, and then went on more freely, having got it out of the way.

"With what the girls make, we figure that the three of us can live very comfortably," he said. "And even old Gollmer may be of some assistance. After all, there are many little things a man like myself can do to make himself helpful around a place."

"What do the girls think of all this?" Miss Finney asked.

"Baba and Lala? They will be happy. They are always happy. Perhaps you do not know. I found them in a very curious place—" He changed his mind, and cut the sentence off. "Sometimes I think they have missed the excitement," he said, "although we have been quite content here. But the girls must have an assured future. Lala is perhaps careless, but Baba is very *sage*, and I think everything will work out quite well."

"There's quite a bit of music and all that stuff in Marseille, isn't there?" Miss Finney said helpfully. "Painting and stuff like that."

"Oh, yes," said Gollmer. "I expect to enjoy the cultural life of the city very much. I must be leaving, Dr. Finney, and thank you."

"Gosh," said Miss Finney. She stood up rather awkwardly, and walked into the room and to the door with Gollmer. There was a moment's dead quiet, then I heard her say, "Well—good luck, Doctor," and I was glad she had used the appellation of honor on him for her last word.

She came back and sat down, rather heavily. Nobody spoke.

Finally I said, "I notice you called him Doctor."

"Oh, hell, that was just a slip," Miss Finney said.

Then again nobody spoke. I sucked up the last of my

lemonade and the straw made a big gurgle in the bottom of the glass.

Emily said tentatively, "Mary—"

"What is it, Emily?"

"That word he used. Mac something."

"You make it sound so Scotch," Miss Finney said, "and it couldn't be more French. *Macareaux*. Men who live off women's earnings."

"I see," said Emily.

"I doubt you do," Miss Finney said. "For instance, if you were married, and your husband lived off what you earn as a missionary, he wouldn't be a *macareau*."

"Oh, but I *do* see," said Emily casually. "You mean prostitutes."

Miss Finney looked at her in a dazed way. "Yes, ma'am," she said. "That's what I mean."

"I thought that was what it was," Emily said, "but I wasn't sure *you* understood." Miss Finney's mouth dropped open and she got it closed again with difficulty. Little Emily sat there for a moment or two, looking out over the river, meditating upon the ways of *macareaux* and their women. Finally she said, in a tone of innocent wisdom:

"Well, why not, if it makes everybody happy?"

"I dunno," Miss Finney managed to say. "I dunno, Emily. Sometimes I really dunno."

Out on the river, the six o'clock launch came into view, very tiny. There was even a sunset back of it. The best seats on the launch are the three right in the stern. It was really too far away, and the water glistened too much, for me to see plainly, but I like to imagine that I saw three figures waving at us from back there.

THE PERENNIAL LIBRARY MYSTERY SERIES

Delano Ames

FOR OLD CRIME'S SAKE *(available 12/82)*   P 629, $2.84

MURDER, MAESTRO, PLEASE *(available 12/82)*   P 630, $2.84
"If there is a more engaging couple in modern fiction than Jane and
Dagobert Brown, we have not met them."   —*Scotsman*

E. C. Bentley

TRENT'S LAST CASE   P 440, $2.50
"One of the three best detective stories ever written."

    —Agatha Christie

TRENT'S OWN CASE   P 516, $2.25
"I won't waste time saying that the plot is sound and the detection
satisfying. Trent has not altered a scrap and reappears with all his old
humor and charm."   —Dorothy L. Sayers

Gavin Black

A DRAGON FOR CHRISTMAS   P 473, $1.95
"Potent excitement!"   —*New York Herald Tribune*

THE EYES AROUND ME   P 485, $1.95
"I stayed up until all hours last night reading *The Eyes Around Me,*
which is something I do not do very often, but I was so intrigued by the
ingeniousness of Mr. Black's plotting and the witty way in which he spins
his mystery. I can only say that I enjoyed the book enormously."

    —F. van Wyck Mason

YOU WANT TO DIE, JOHNNY?   P 472, $1.95
"Gavin Black doesn't just develop a pressure plot in suspense, he adds
uninfected wit, character, charm, and sharp knowledge of the Far East
to make rereading as keen as the first race-through."   —*Book Week*

Nicholas Blake

THE CORPSE IN THE SNOWMAN   P 427, $1.95
"If there is a distinction between the novel and the detective story (which
we do not admit), then this book deserves a high place in both catego-
ries."   —*The New York Times*

THE WIDOW'S CRUISE   P 399, $2.25
"A stirring suspense.... The thrilling tale leaves nothing to be desired."
                                          —*Springfield Republican*

THE WORM OF DEATH   P 400, $2.25
"It [The Worm of Death] is one of Blake's very best—and his best is
better than almost anyone's."   —Louis Untermeyer

John & Emery Bonett

A BANNER FOR PEGASUS   P 554, $2.40
"A gem! Beautifully plotted and set.... Not only is the murder adroit
and deserved, and the detection competent, but the love story is charming."   —Jacques Barzun and Wendell Hertig Taylor

DEAD LION   P 563, $2.40
"A clever plot, authentic background and interesting characters highly
recommended this one."   —*New Republic*

Christianna Brand

GREEN FOR DANGER   P 551, $2.50
"You have to reach for the greatest of Great Names (Christie, Carr,
Queen ...) to find Brand's rivals in the devious subtleties of the trade."
                                          —Anthony Boucher

TOUR DE FORCE   P 572, $2.40
"Complete with traps for the over-ingenious, a double-reverse surprise
ending and a key clue planted so fairly and obviously that you completely
overlook it. If that's your idea of perfect entertainment, then seize at once
upon *Tour de Force.*"   —Anthony Boucher, *The New York Times*

James Byrom

OR BE HE DEAD   P 585, $2.84
"A very original tale ... Well written and steadily entertaining."
  —Jacques Barzun & Wendell Hertig Taylor, *A Catalogue of Crime*

Marjorie Carleton

VANISHED   P 559, $2.40
"Exceptional ... a minor triumph."
  —Jacques Barzun and Wendell Hertig Taylor, *A Catalogue of Crime*

George Harmon Coxe

MURDER WITH PICTURES   P 527, $2.25
"[Coxe] has hit the bull's-eye with his first shot."
                                        —*The New York Times*

Edmund Crispin

BURIED FOR PLEASURE   P 506, $2.50
"Absolute and unalloyed delight."
                    —Anthony Boucher, *The New York Times*

Lionel Davidson

THE MENORAH MEN   P 592, $2.84
"Of his fellow thriller writers, only John Le Carré shows the same
instinct for the viscera."   —*Chicago Tribune*

NIGHT OF WENCESLAS   P 595, $2.84
"A most ingenious thriller, so enriched with style, wit, and a sense of
serious comedy that it all but transcends its kind."
                                         —*The New Yorker*

THE ROSE OF TIBET   P 593, $2.84
"I hadn't realized how much I missed the genuine Adventure story
. . . until I read *The Rose of Tibet*."   —Graham Greene

D. M. Devine

MY BROTHER'S KILLER   P 558, $2.40
"A most enjoyable crime story which I enjoyed reading down to the last
moment."   —Agatha Christie

Kenneth Fearing

THE BIG CLOCK   P 500, $1.95
"It will be some time before chill-hungry clients meet again so rare a
compound of irony, satire, and icy-fingered narrative. *The Big Clock* is
. . . a psychothriller you won't put down."   —*Weekly Book Review*

Andrew Garve

THE ASHES OF LODA   P 430, $1.50
"Garve . . . embellishes a fine fast adventure story with a more credible
picture of the U.S.S.R. than is offered in most thrillers."
                              —*The New York Times Book Review*

THE CUCKOO LINE AFFAIR P 451, $1.95

". . . an agreeable and ingenious piece of work." —*The New Yorker*

A HERO FOR LEANDA P 429, $1.50

"One can trust Mr. Garve to put a fresh twist to any situation, and the ending is really a lovely surprise." —*The Manchester Guardian*

MURDER THROUGH THE LOOKING GLASS P 449, $1.95

". . . refreshingly out-of-the-way and enjoyable . . . highly recommended to all comers." —*Saturday Review*

NO TEARS FOR HILDA P 441, $1.95

"It starts fine and finishes finer. I got behind on breathing watching Max get not only his man but his woman, too." —Rex Stout

THE RIDDLE OF SAMSON P 450, $1.95

"The story is an excellent one, the people are quite likable, and the writing is superior." —*Springfield Republican*

Michael Gilbert

BLOOD AND JUDGMENT P 446, $1.95

"Gilbert readers need scarcely be told that the characters all come alive at first sight, and that his surpassing talent for narration enhances any plot. . . . Don't miss." —*San Francisco Chronicle*

THE BODY OF A GIRL P 459, $1.95

"Does what a good mystery should do: open up into all kinds of ramifications, with untold menace behind the action. At the end, there is a bang-up climax, and it is a pleasure to see how skilfully Gilbert wraps everything up." —*The New York Times Book Review*

THE DANGER WITHIN P 448, $1.95

"Michael Gilbert has nicely combined some elements of the straight detective story with plenty of action, suspense, and adventure, to produce a superior thriller." —*Saturday Review*

FEAR TO TREAD P 458, $1.95

"Merits serious consideration as a work of art."

—*The New York Times*

Joe Gores

HAMMETT P 631, $2.84

"Joe Gores at his very best. Terse, powerful writing—with the master, Dashiell Hammett, as the protagonist in a novel I think he would have been proud to call his own." —Robert Ludlum

C. W. Grafton

BEYOND A REASONABLE DOUBT P 519, $1.95
"A very ingenious tale of murder . . . a brilliant and gripping narrative."
—Jacques Barzun and Wendell Hertig Taylor

Edward Grierson

THE SECOND MAN P 528, $2.25
"One of the best trial-testimony books to have come along in quite a while." —The New Yorker

Cyril Hare

DEATH IS NO SPORTSMAN P 555, $2.40
"You will be thrilled because it succeeds in placing an ingenious story in a new and refreshing setting. . . . The identity of the murderer is really a surprise." —Daily Mirror

DEATH WALKS THE WOODS P 556, $2.40
"Here is a fine formal detective story, with a technically brilliant solution demanding the attention of all connoisseurs of construction."
—Anthony Boucher, The New York Times Book Review

AN ENGLISH MURDER P 455, $2.50
"By a long shot, the best crime story I have read for a long time. Everything is traditional, but originality does not suffer. The setting is perfect. Full marks to Mr. Hare." —Irish Press

TENANT FOR DEATH P 570, $2.84
"The way in which an air of probability is combined both with clear, terse narrative and with a good deal of subtle suburban atmosphere, proves the extreme skill of the writer." —The Spectator

TRAGEDY AT LAW P 522, $2.25
"An extremely urbane and well-written detective story."
—The New York Times

UNTIMELY DEATH P 514, $2.25
"The English detective story at its quiet best, meticulously underplayed, rich in perceivings of the droll human animal and ready at the last with a neat surprise which has been there all the while had we but wits to see it." —New York Herald Tribune Book Review

THE WIND BLOWS DEATH P 589, $2.84
"A plot compounded of musical knowledge, a Dickens allusion, and a subtle point in law is related with delightfully unobtrusive wit, warmth, and style." —The New York Times

Elspeth Huxley

THE AFRICAN POISON MURDERS P 540, $2.25
"Obscure venom, manical mutilations, deadly bush fire, thrilling climax compose major opus.... Top-flight."
—*Saturday Review of Literature*

MURDER ON SAFARI P 587, $2.84
"Right now we'd call Mrs. Huxley a dangerous rival to Agatha Christie." —*Books*

Francis Iles

BEFORE THE FACT P 517, $2.50
"Not many 'serious' novelists have produced character studies to compare with Iles's internally terrifying portrait of the murderer in *Before the Fact,* his masterpiece and a work truly deserving the appellation of unique and beyond price." —Howard Haycraft

MALICE AFORETHOUGHT P 532, $1.95
"It is a long time since I have read anything so good as *Malice Aforethought,* with its cynical humour, acute criminology, plausible detail and rapid movement. It makes you hug yourself with pleasure."
—H. C. Harwood, *Saturday Review*

Michael Innes

DEATH BY WATER P 574, $2.40
"The amount of ironic social criticism and deft characterization of scenes and people would serve another author for six books."
—Jacques Barzun and Wendell Hertig Taylor

HARE SITTING UP P 590, $2.84
"There is hardly anyone (in mysteries or mainstream) more exquisitely literate, allusive and Jamesian—and hardly anyone with a firmer sense of melodramatic plot or a more vigorous gift of storytelling."
—Anthony Boucher, *The New York Times*

THE LONG FAREWELL P 575, $2.40
"A model of the deft, classic detective story, told in the most wittily diverting prose." —*The New York Times*

THE MAN FROM THE SEA P 591, $2.84
"The pace is brisk, the adventures exciting and excitingly told, and above all he keeps to the very end the interesting ambiguity of the man from the sea." —*New Statesman*

Michael Innes (cont'd)

THE SECRET VANGUARD   P 584, $2.84

"Innes . . . has mastered the art of swift, exciting and well-organized narrative."
         —The New York Times

Mary Kelly

THE SPOILT KILL   P 565, $2.40

"Mary Kelly is a new Dorothy Sayers. . . . [An] exciting new novel."
         —Evening News

Lange Lewis

THE BIRTHDAY MURDER   P 518, $1.95

"Almost perfect in its playlike purity and delightful prose."
         —Jacques Barzun and Wendell Hertig Taylor

Allan MacKinnon

HOUSE OF DARKNESS   P 582, $2.84

"His best . . . a perfect compendium."
         —Jacques Barzun & Wendell Hertig Taylor, *A Catalogue of Crime*

Arthur Maling

LUCKY DEVIL   P 482, $1.95

"The plot unravels at a fast clip, the writing is breezy and Maling's approach is as fresh as today's stockmarket quotes."
         —Louisville Courier Journal

RIPOFF   P 483, $1.95

"A swiftly paced story of today's big business is larded with intrigue as a Ralph Nader-type investigates an insurance scandal and is soon on the run from a hired gun and his brother. . . . Engrossing and credible."
         —Booklist

SCHROEDER'S GAME   P 484, $1.95

"As the title indicates, this Schroeder is up to something, and the unravelling of his game is a diverting and sufficiently blood-soaked entertainment."
         —The New Yorker

Austin Ripley

MINUTE MYSTERIES   P 387, $2.50

More than one hundred of the world's shortest detective stories. Only one possible solution to each case!

Thomas Sterling

THE EVIL OF THE DAY   P 529, $2.50
"Prose as witty and subtle as it is sharp and clear. . .characters unconventionally conceived and richly bodied forth . . . . In short, a novel to be treasured.".   —Anthony Boucher, *The New York Times*

Julian Symons

THE BELTING INHERITANCE   P 468, $1.95
"A superb whodunit in the best tradition of the detective story."
                      —August Derleth, *Madison Capital Times*

BLAND BEGINNING   P 469, $1.95
"Mr. Symons displays a deft storytelling skill, a quiet and literate wit, a nice feeling for character, and detectival ingenuity of a high order."
                      —Anthony Boucher, *The New York Times*

BOGUE'S FORTUNE   P 481, $1.95
"There's a touch of the old sardonic humour, and more than a touch of style."   —*The Spectator*

THE BROKEN PENNY   P 480, $1.95
"The most exciting, astonishing and believable spy story to appear in years.   —Anthony Boucher, *The New York Times Book Review*

THE COLOR OF MURDER   P 461, $1.95
"A singularly unostentatious and memorably brilliant detective story."
                      —*New York Herald Tribune Book Review*

Dorothy Stockbridge Tillet
(John Stephen Strange)

THE MAN WHO KILLED FORTESCUE   P 536, $2.25
"Better than average."   —*Saturday Review of Literature*

Simon Troy

THE ROAD TO RHUINE   P 583, $2.84
"Unusual and agreeably told."   —*San Francisco Chronicle*

SWIFT TO ITS CLOSE   P 546, $2.40
"A nicely literate British mystery . . . the atmosphere and the plot are exceptionally well wrought, the dialogue excellent."   —*Best Sellers*

Henry Wade

THE DUKE OF YORK'S STEPS   P 588, $2.84
"A classic of the golden age."
>—Jacques Barzun & Wendell Hertig Taylor, *A Catalogue of Crime*

A DYING FALL   P 543, $2.50
"One of those expert British suspense jobs . . . it crackles with undercurrents of blackmail, violent passion and murder. Topnotch in its class."
>—*Time*

THE HANGING CAPTAIN   P 548, $2.50
"This is a detective story for connoisseurs, for those who value clear thinking and good writing above mere ingenuity and easy thrills."
>—*Times Literary Supplement*

Hillary Waugh

LAST SEEN WEARING . . .   P 552, $2.40
"A brilliant tour de force."   —Julian Symons

THE MISSING MAN   P 553, $2.40
"The quiet detailed police work of Chief Fred C. Fellows, Stockford, Conn., is at its best in *The Missing Man* . . . one of the Chief's toughest cases and one of the best handled."
>—Anthony Boucher, *The New York Times Book Review*

Henry Kitchell Webster

WHO IS THE NEXT?   P 539, $2.25
"A double murder, private-plane piloting, a neat impersonation, and a delicate courtship are adroitly combined by a writer who knows how to use the language."   —Jacques Barzun and Wendell Hertig Taylor

Anna Mary Wells

MURDERER'S CHOICE   P 534, $2.50
"Good writing, ample action, and excellent character work."
>—*Saturday Review of Literature*

A TALENT FOR MURDER   P 535, $2.25
"The discovery of the villain is a decided shock."   —*Books*

Edward Young

THE FIFTH PASSENGER   P 544, $2.25
"Clever and adroit . . . excellent thriller . . ."   —*Library Journal*

If you enjoyed this book you'll want to know about THE PERENNIAL LIBRARY MYSTERY SERIES

Buy them at your local bookstore or use this coupon for ordering:

Qty	P number	Price

	postage and handling charge	$1.00
	_____ book(s) @ $0.25	
	TOTAL	

Prices contained in this coupon are Harper & Row invoice prices only. They are subject to change without notice, and in no way reflect the prices at which these books may be sold by other suppliers.

HARPER & ROW, Mail Order Dept. #PMS, 10 East 53rd St., New York, N.Y. 10022.

Please send me the books I have checked above. I am enclosing $_____ which includes a postage and handling charge of $1.00 for the first book and 25¢ for each additional book. Send check or money order. No cash or C.O.D.s please

Name_____

Address_____

City_____ State_____ Zip_____

Please allow 4 weeks for delivery. USA only. This offer expires 11/30/83
Please add applicable sales tax.